The Man
Who Wasn't There

Also by Pat Barker

Union Street

Blow Your House Down

Liza's England (formerly entitled *The Century's Daughter*)

The Regeneration Trilogy

Regeneration

The Eye in the Door

The Ghost Road

Another World

Border Crossing

The Man
Who Wasn't There

PAT BARKER

Picador USA
New York

Picador® is a U.S. registered trademark and is used by St. Martin's Press under license from Pan Books Limited.

For information on Picador USA Reading Group Guides, as well as ordering, please contact the Trade Marketing department at St. Martin's Press.
Phone: 1-800-221-7945 extension 763
Fax: 212-677-7456
E-mail: trademarketing@stmartins.com

ISBN 0-312-27543-9

First published in Great Britain by Virago Press

First Picador USA Edition: April 2001

10 9 8 7 6 5 4 3 2 1

For David

Thursday

1

Colin Harper, one eye open for snipers, turned the corner into his own road. You were supposed to walk down the middle, but the last time he'd done that Blenkinsop's dad had honked his horn and shouted, 'Get off the road, you stupid little bugger!'

The houses were tall and narrow, set back from the road behind low walls whose railings, pulled up in the last war to make Spitfires, had never been replaced. Before the war, his nan said, entire houses had been lived in by just one family, but now they were divided into flats, or turned into boarding houses. Not very successful boarding houses. Most of the notices he passed said *Vacancies*: they were too far away from the sea to be easily filled, especially in September.

Colin plodded up the hill, half moons of sweat in the armpits of his grey shirt. In the distance, lampposts and parked cars shimmered in the heat. All around him was the smell of hot tar.

Gaston jerks himself awake. A sniper is crawling across Blenkinsop's roof, but Gaston has seen him. He spins round, levels the gun, and *fires*.

The sniper – slow motion now – clutches his chest, buckles at the knee, crashes in an endlessly unfurling fountain of glass through the roof of Mr Blenkinsop's greenhouse, where he lands face down, his fingers clutching the damp earth – and his chest squashing Mr Blenkinsop's prize tomatoes.

Gaston blows nonchalantly across the smoking metal of his gun, and, with never a backward glance, strides up the garden path and into the house.

As he passes through the hall, Gaston taps the face of a brass barometer, as if to persuade it to change its mind. No use. The needle points, as it does unswervingly, in all weathers, to Rain. Madame Hennigan, the landlady, believes in being realistic, and no mere barometer is permitted to disagree.

Gaston clatters up the uncarpeted stairs to the top-floor flat.

Where he becomes, abruptly, Colin again.

'Where the bloody hell have you been?' Viv asked. 'I thought I told you I wanted you back in before I go out?'

'I got kept in. And anyway, I am back.'

'You're always getting kept in.'

'Not my fault.'

'Aw no, it couldn't be. Well, you can get your own tea, I'm not doing it.'

'I always do.'

'You poor little sod.'

Colin went through into the kitchen, where a tin of baked beans stood by the gas cooker. He put his head round the kitchen door. 'Beans again? I'm sick of bloody beans.'

'Then you'd better learn to cook summat else.'

'Farting Fenwick ought to live here.'

'Who's that?'

He could tell by her voice she wasn't interested. 'Lad in our class. He can fart "God Save the Queen".'

'That must please the teachers.'

'Last time he did it Miss Campbell burst into tears.'

'I've no sympathy,' said Viv. 'None whatsoever. If they took the stick to you a bit more often, 'stead of all this keeping you in, they might get somewhere.'

''S not *me*. I'd shove a cork up his bum as soon as anybody. I got *kept in* because you still haven't signed me report.'

'What's to stop you signing it?'

'It's supposed to be your signature.'

Viv turned to him. 'So forge the bugger.'

'You haven't even read it yet.'

Viv sighed. 'Look, love, just let me finish getting ready, and I promise you I'll read it. OK?'

'OK.'

Colin put two slices of bread under the grill, poured the beans into a pan, and began to stir.

'Is that a wooden spoon you're using?'

'Yes, Mam.'

'Good. Only I don't want them saucepans scraped.'

The doorbell chimed.

'That'll be Pauline.'

Pauline was Viv's best friend. They worked in one of the nightclubs that had sprung up along the coast road, 'glorified waitresses' Viv said, though they were dressed as fawns.

'Give me ears a quick steam, will you, pet?'

'I'm watching the toast.'

Steaming Viv's ears was a nightly job. Fawns with bedraggled ears got into trouble, and Viv couldn't afford trouble. Thirty-six was over the hill, for a fawn.

Pauline came in. 'Hiya, Viv. Hello, Colin.'

'I won't be a minute,' Viv said. 'He's just doing me ears. I think.'

'No rush.' Pauline settled herself into the armchair. 'And how's Colin?'

'All right.'

'He got kept in again.'

Pauline smiled. 'You been a bad lad?'

'No.'

'No, it's all my fault apparently. A mother's place is in the wrong.'

'You should hear the two little bitches I've just left. Half-starved, nothing to wear. You'd think they were walking down the street with nowt to cover their bums.'

'Your ears.' Colin dumped them on the table.

'Beats me why men fancy women with fluffy ears,' said Pauline.

'They don't,' Viv said. 'They wouldn't bring their wives with them if they were fancying.'

'Oh, the wives.'

'I know what you mean. Bloody beady little eyes all over you. Give me a fella any day.'

'Are you gunna read me report?'

Viv waved her fingernails. 'When I've finished drying me varnish, yes.'

'Can *I* have a look, Colin?'

Colin gave Pauline the report, though he couldn't see why she would want to read it.

'They don't half do some funny things at that school. Al . . . Al . . . What is it?'

'Algebra.' Colin was watching Viv. 'It's sums . . . sort of.'

Viv laughed. 'It's not *sort-of* sums *you* need. It's the sort that stops you getting diddled. Do you know, I sent him out with a quid to buy a loaf of bread and a jar of jam and he came back with one and six? I says "What's that?" He says, "It's all she give me." I says, "You get yourself back there, and tell her you give her a quid." It was her at the bottom, you know. Her with the blue rinse.'

'Ooh she's very sharp, her. Did you get it back?'

'Yes.'

'Aye, this time. But he mightn't always be as lucky.' Viv screwed the top back on the nail varnish. 'He's in a dream.'

Pauline shrugged. 'We've all got to learn. How old are you, Colin?'

'Twelve.'

''S a nice age, that.' She raised her voice to carry across the room. 'You want to make the most of it, you know, Viv. Last little bit of calm before the storm.'

'I thought this was the storm.'

'Don't you believe it. Fifteen's the storm.'

Viv looked at Colin. 'Oh, all right, give it here.'

'You've got a bright lad there. You want to be proud of him.'

'Oh, he's sharp enough . . .'

'A bright lad and a bonny lad, eh, Colin?'

'Sharp enough to cut hisself.' Viv glanced down the report. 'I just wish I could see the point of a lot of it. Latin: *Very fair*. English: *I enjoy reading his stories*.'

'He's getting an education, isn't he, that's the point. I just wished I'd had the opportunity. I wouldn't be stuck in that dump putting lead in pencils for a living.'

'You don't put lead in pencils,' Colin said.

'Not always I don't, son. You're right there.'

Colin blushed, realizing what she meant a second too late.

''Course, his dad was bright,' Viv said, pushing her hair into shape. 'I think.'

'Bright enough to bugger off,' Colin said.

Viv turned on him. 'He didn't bugger off, Colin. He was shot down.'

Pauline busied herself with straightening the seams of her nylons.

'When you going to tell me about him?'

'When you're old enough.'

'And when will that be?'

'I don't know, do I? Twenty-one.'

'Aw Mam.'

'Never mind, "*Aw Mam*".' Viv turned back to her reflection. 'Dunno why I bother.'

'You look all right,' Pauline said.

'Mind, you look at them you wonder why any of us bother.'

'What you doing tonight, Colin?' Pauline asked.

'Dunno. Going to the pictures.'

'You got enough money?' Viv asked.

'I could do with ten bob.'

'When couldn't you?' Viv handed him the note. 'And I don't want you running the streets till all hours, either. I want you back home, in bed, *asleep*, by the time I get back.'

Pauline ruffled Colin's hair as she walked past. 'See you.'

Outside, in the passage, Viv said, 'You can't keep your hands off him, can you?'

'I'm in training to be a mucky old woman.'

'Talent like yours, love, you shouldn't need training.'

He heard the tap of their heels on the lino, and a click as the front door closed.

2

As soon as he was sure they'd gone, Colin ran upstairs to his mother's room. He hesitated in the doorway, but only for a second.

—*Course, his dad was bright. I think.*

—*Bright enough to bugger off.*

—*He didn't bugger off, Colin. He was shot down.*

Colin sniffed, identifying the various smells in the room. Amami setting lotion, Pond's cold cream, the crumbly, purple mothballs Viv put in the pockets of her winter coat.

—*When you going to tell me about him?*

—*When you're old enough.*

—And when will that be?

—I don't know, do I? Twenty-one.

'Not bloody likely. I want to know now.'

The wardrobe was the likeliest place. He opened the door, pushed the heavy coats aside, and there, at the bottom, behind a row of shoes, was a battered, brown handbag. It was so old the leather had split in places, and the canvas backing showed through. He knelt down and took it out.

Every compartment was stuffed full of papers. Colin pulled off his school sweater, threw it across the foot of the bed, and tipped them all out on to the floor.

He'd seen his birth certificate, of course. The shorter version. On his first day at Queen Elizabeth's, they'd all had to take their birth certificates to show the headmaster . . .

They had to go out to the front, one row at a time, and queue to show their certificates.

On the blackboard, in capital letters, were words Colin couldn't understand, though he recognized some names: Pierre, Gaston, Maurice, and guessed the language was French. He moved his lips, as he waited, trying to imagine the strange sounds.

When he'd arrived at school that morning, he'd been worried, because Viv had insisted on buying his blazer several sizes too big. Plenty of room, she called it. But now, when he looked round the classroom, he could see that everybody's blazer was too big, so that was all right.

The boy in front had a larger certificate than his. Colin peered over the boy's shoulder, and saw the name of his father: Gilbert Reid.

He looked down at his own certificate. It gave only his own name, and the date and place of his birth. March 5th, 1943. Scarpington. Feeling slightly uneasy, he looked at the boy behind, and then at the boy behind *him*, and so on down the line. All of them had the long certificate.

Except one boy, right at the end, who met Colin's eye, and looked away.

It was all right, nothing unpleasant happened. Mr Sawdon took the certificate, checked the information against the register, even smiled as he handed it back. But underneath the smile, Colin thought he detected a flicker of . . . Something else. Curiosity? Whatever it was, it wasn't there when he looked at the other boys.

Remembering that look, Colin sighed. He thought, *It's no use, I'll never find it.* After all, he couldn't even be sure it existed, perhaps he just didn't have one, but then he reached for the next bundle of papers, and there it was.

Very slowly, he unfolded the thick paper and smoothed the creases out. His own name and sex, Viv's name and occupation, and then:

Name and surname of father: _____
Rank or Profession of father: _____

Colin stared at the lines of black ink, even ran his finger across them, as if willing them to disgorge words.

He thought: *It doesn't matter.* After all, whoever his father had been, *he* was still the same person, it made no difference to *him.* And all the while he thought this, he knew it did matter.

A RAILWAY STATION IN FRANCE. MARCH 1943

The steam from a train clears to reveal German guards waiting at the barrier.

German soldiers, the majority of the travellers, come and go freely, but French civilians must queue to present their identification papers. Housewives, young girls, an old man, a priest, and several schoolboys – wearing the maroon-and-gold blazer of Queen Elizabeth's Grammar school. All, in turn, present their identity cards for inspection, and, after a slow, careful checking, all are waved through.

Two faces stand out from the rest. One, a young boy, Gaston, an orphan on his way to join his uncle. Or, at least, this is what his identity papers say. Only a slight twitching of the muscles round the eyes betrays an inner tension and suggests that the identity papers he holds out so confidently are false.

The other is a young man at the back of the queue.

Von Strohm, head of the Gestapo in this region, and, in another time and place, the headmaster of an English grammar school, watches closely as the guard returns the papers.

Gaston walks on, not looking back, but he's clearly interested in the fate of the young man at the back of the queue, whose face, as he comes closer to the barrier, begins to glisten with sweat.

GASTON
(*under his breath*)

C'mon, c'mon, it's all right.

But the man at the back of the queue is beyond help. His eyes focus on the gloved hand of the guard reaching out to take the identity papers of the woman in front, and, with a sudden tearing of the nerves, he runs.

GUARD

Achtung! Achtung!

Rifle-fire cracks out, French civilians scatter, and the man throws up his arms, caught like a runner breasting the tape, and held there for a moment, before he, slowly, falls.

Von Strohm turns away from this death. He's already watching the faces of the other civilians, looking for the one face that betrays excessive fear. Gaston meets von Strohm's eyes, calmly. They hold one another's gaze.

High above, pigeons, alarmed by the shots, beat their wings against the glass roof, bewildered by the solidity of air. The clapping of their wings echoes round and round the roof of the station . . .

and fades on the window of Viv Harper's bedroom.

Colin shivered as the room took shape around him again. He put his birth certificate back into the handbag, and closed the wardrobe door.

3

Adrian Hennigan ran his fingers through his hair and smiled at his reflection in the glass. 'What you see before you,' he said, 'is some bint's lucky night.'

Mrs Hennigan shrieked her appreciation, and even her next-door neighbour, Mrs Hinde, managed a thin smile.

'You'll have to get summat else on though, won't you?' she said.

Adrian was still wearing his work trousers and shirt.

'Missus,' Adrian said, turning from the mirror, 'it's not the clothes that make the man. I . . .' He raised his index finger, '. . . have a secret weapon.'

The women dissolved into giggles. Adrian grinned at Colin, who was curled up in a corner of the sofa. 'Colin, there is nowt worse than a mucky-minded woman. Here.' With a mock-effeminate gesture, Adrian unbuttoned his cuff, rolled back his sleeve and put his wrist to Colin's nose. 'How's that for Evening in Paris?'

Colin pulled a face. 'Ugh.'

'You wanna know what that is, son? That is lions' . . .' He glanced at Mrs Hinde, '. . . *widdle*.'

'It never is,' said Mrs Hinde.

''S true as I stand here. I'd just gone over to have a chat with Johnny Stewart and I was stood with me back to the cage, you know – watching the odd bit of talent go past – when all of a sudden, up he gets – Caesar, this is – *strolls* across the cage, points his bum in my direction and . . . pssssss . . . All over me. Well, I had to go and get washed, didn't I? And then – this is luck for you – what does the headkeeper do? He decides he'll go and have a look at the lions. "Where's Hennigan?" Well, of course, that daft bugger Stewart *told* him. Oh, and you should've heard him go on. "If you was close enough to get pissed on, son, you was close enough to get mauled. I've warned you before," he says. "You're supposed to be a keeper, not a bloody lion-tamer." I says, "But I'm part of his territory, aren't I? He's bound to want to . . . widdle on me. But you know, that's the difference. Some folks think as long as you're shoving food through the bars and mucking 'em out, you're doing a good job, but you're not. You've gotta *think* like them.'

'You don't half pong,' Colin said.

Adrian looked disgusted. 'Well, of course I do.'

'I thought there was something when I come in,' said Mrs Hinde, glancing at Mrs Hennigan. 'But I didn't like to say.'

'Powerful stuff this, Missus. You should see what it does to the lionesses.' Adrian leant over Mrs Hinde, and roared.

Mrs Hennigan laughed, but Colin thought she looked worried. A few years ago Adrian had been in constant trouble with the police. Even National Service, which Mrs Hennigan had hoped would sort him out, didn't. He got to know every rogue in the Army, and kept in touch with them all. Within a few weeks of his discharge, the police were again knocking at the door.

'It's not my lad you want to be looking for,' Mrs Hennigan told them. 'It's that Brian Combey.'

Despite Mrs Hennigan's advice, the police arrested Adrian. This time it was prison, though not a long sentence. With remission for good behaviour, he'd only served three months.

While Adrian was inside, Brian Combey did a warehouse job. The security guard, who'd been chasing him across the roof, slipped, and broke his back. Combey got three years.

Adrian came back to find the neighbourhood a quieter place. But then, Adrian himself seemed changed. He sat in his room and brooded, going out only at weekends and then coming home so drunk that he sometimes collapsed on the stairs and lay there till morning. 'I don't know what happened to him in that prison,' Mrs Hennigan said 'But it must've been something awful.'

This went on for several months. Then the probation officer found him a job at the zoo. '*Mucking out*?' the neighbours said. 'He'll never stick that.'

But they'd been proved wrong.

Cautiously at first, Mrs Hennigan began to hope. The police no longer knocked at her door. She was happier, and better off, now, than she had been for years, and if, tonight, she seemed a little worried, it could only be because Brian Combey was back. Mrs Merrill had seen him, or so she said, walking along the coast road, cropped head bent into the driving rain. That had been yesterday morning. But Adrian had said nothing, and yet if Brian Combey had been released, Adrian must know.

Mrs Hennigan's eyes followed her son as he walked across the room and got a bucket from under the kitchen sink. He turned to Colin and said, 'Gunna feed the hens for me?'

'Yeah, I don't mind.'

Adrian ruffled his hair. 'Good on yer, mate.'

Mrs Hinde turned to stare at Adrian. '*Hens*. You'll have to make your mind up what you're doing with them.'

The 'hens' were Adrian's latest venture. Certain snakes in the reptile house had to be fed living prey, and day-old chicks were the answer. Day-old cocks, to be precise, but since the sexing of chicks is notoriously unreliable, Adrian reckoned that at least half those he carried home in his pocket – whispering 'python' and 'boa constrictor' to them every time they cheeped – would turn out to be hens.

Ever since then Mrs Hinde had been peering over the wall that divided the two back gardens, and as the chicks grew so did her suspicions.

Now, she said, 'I don't like to say this, Adrian, but they're all . . .' Her lips puckered. 'Cocks.'

Adrian went on mixing the feed.

'And the big one's started crowing. It'll not be long before the others join in. To say nothing of fight.'

Silence.

'You can't expect people putting up with that, you know, Adrian. This is a residential neighbourhood.'

Adrian turned. 'What do you want me to do, Missus? Go outside and wring their necks?'

'No need for that kind of talk,' said Mrs Hennigan with a glance at Colin. 'Do you know he's got names for them all?'

'Aye,' said Adrian. 'And what names. *Rosie*. My God. Poor little bugger blushes every time he looks at me.'

'Not so little,' said Mrs Hinde.

'No, he's a good big bird,' said Mrs Hennigan.

'Can you eat cocks?' asked Mrs Hinde.

'Dunno, Missus,' said Adrian, 'but you could have a lot of fun trying.'

'*Adrian!*'

Adrian turned back to the sink.

'You're not really gunna wring their necks, are you?' asked Colin, going across to get the bucket.

'No. I'll think of something.'

He didn't sound very sure. Colin went out into the sunshine, rattling the spoon against the side of the bucket, and all the young cocks came running, necks outstretched towards him. He scattered the meal, throwing it out in wide arcs, and the screeching died to a contented clucking, as they began to scratch and peck the dust.

Rosie, the oldest and biggest, the one whose crowing disturbed the neighbourhood, came towards him, stepping delicately on cracked feet. He paused, one spurred foot curled over onto itself. His feathers were gold, pure gold, darkening to black and inky green around the tail, and his coxcomb, where the sun shone through it, was a brilliant, ruby red. The same colour, Colin thought, as your fingers are when you cup them round a torch.

A sour smell came from the shed behind him, a smell of dust and stale shit. Colin thought of golden feathers bedraggled in death, of bright eyes glazed and dying, and the sunshine blackened all around him, and he was glad to get inside.

One hand on the knob of the living-room door, he stopped.

'I see she still goes out and leaves him every night,' Mrs Hinde was saying.

'He's a big lad,' said Adrian. 'He can take care of himself.'

'Aye, now he can,' Mrs Hennigan said. 'But she was going out and leaving him when he was only six.'

'What is it she calls herself?' said Mrs Hinde. 'A waitress?'

'That's right,' said Mrs Hennigan.

Mrs Hinde laughed. 'Not what they called it in our young day.'

'Yackety-yak-yak,' Adrian said. 'Leave some skin on the poor woman's back, can't you?'

Colin opened the door and walked in.

'Eeh,' Mrs Hinde said. 'Is that the time?'

'Yes,' said Adrian.

'He'll be hollering for his grub.'

'What, already?' said Mrs Hennigan. 'I thought you'd just give him his tea.'

'Ah, but you see the trouble is with him having no stomach he can't take very much. The doctor says, "A little and often, Mrs Hinde," but he never said how little and how often.'

When Mrs Hennigan came back from seeing Mrs Hinde out, she said, 'You're awful with that woman, Adrian, and I'm sure I don't know why. She's had a lot of trouble in her life.'

Adrian had gone to the sink and was rinsing out the bucket. 'Caused a fair bit 'n' all.'

Mrs Hennigan sat beside Colin. 'What you doing tonight, son?'

'Going to the pictures.'

'Aw smashing, eh?' She raised her voice. 'Adrian?'

'Yeah?'

Mrs Hennigan said, 'It's just Colin wondered if you could give him a lift. If you're taking the bike.'

'Yeah, sure. Where to, Colin?'

Colin was aware of being used, and didn't like it. 'The Odeon.'

'That won't be out of your way, will it, Adrian?'

'Ma,' Adrian rested one finger on the end of his nose. 'Keep it out.'

'I just thought you might be going to the Feathers, that's all.'

'And what if I am? Mam, I'm twenty-two.'

She watched him put his jacket on. 'He's out again, isn't he?'

'Who is?'

'Aw *Adrian*.'

Adrian flicked a speck of imaginary dandruff from his shoulder. 'You know as much as I do, Ma.'

'You mean you haven't seen him?'

Adrian hesitated. 'Not to speak to, no.'

'But you have seen him?'

'Look, he drinks in the Feathers, Mam. I'm not changing my pub to suit Brian. Or you.'

'He's not been inside five minutes.'

'He's done his time.'

'Three years for a man's back. It was nowt.'

'Look, Mam, Brian was nowhere near that bloke when he fell. Everybody accepted that. Even the prosecution accepted it. And anyway what was he doing chasing across the roof? T'wasn't his stuff.'

'He was doing his *job*.' She waited for him to speak. 'Brian can do no wrong with you, can he? You think the sun shines out of his arse.'

'No, I don't.'

'Aw, go on, Adrian, tell the truth.'

'You don't give up on your mates just because they've had a bit of bad luck.'

'*Bad luck*?'

But Adrian had already left the room. Mrs Hennigan sat by the empty grate, her fingers pleating and unpleating the hem of her skirt. Colin had gone very quiet.

Just as they'd both given up hope of Adrian returning the door opened. 'Ready, Col?'

Colin felt in his pockets for his money.

'No need to wait up, Mam,' Adrian said. 'I've got me key.'

'I wasn't going to, son.'

Colin followed Adrian into the back garden. Before the

arrival of Rosie, Elsie and the rest, Adrian's bike had been kept in the shed. Now it stood on the path, shrouded in tarpaulins, on a slick of its own grease.

Adrian bundled the covers into a corner, sat astride the bike, and began heaving it backwards into the cobbled alley that ran behind the house. His foot kicked, once, twice, and the engine exploded.

'Odeon?' Adrian yelled above the roar.

'Yeah,' said Colin. 'But anywhere on the front'll do.'

Colin climbed on, wrapped his arms round Adrian's chest, and pressed his cheek into his jacket. The bike leapt forward. Ahead of them a line of washing hung low, but Adrian took the bike underneath, crouching between the handlebars. Wet sheets clipped their cheeks and hair as they roared through.

Adrian's foot came out, groping the cobbles. Then they were hurtling along Wellington Street, and out on to the coast road where tiny, stinging particles of sand whipped their faces. Colin peered round Adrian's shoulder, but the wind ballooned his cheeks until he gagged, and hid his face against Adrian's back again.

When they reached the front, Adrian slowed to a crawl to avoid the day-trippers who crowded the narrow road. A smell of brine and vinegar came from the shrimp booths, though their wooden shutters were closed. Adrian pulled into the kerb.

'Here, all right?'

'Fine.' Colin got off the bike, knees wobbling from the excitement of the ride. 'See you then.'

Adrian clipped him affectionately on the side of the head. 'Yeah, see you.'

Colin stood on the gritty pavement watching until Adrian was out of sight. He had his hand raised to wave, but Adrian didn't look back.

4

A gang of teenage boys had gathered on the steps of the
Odeon. Boys Colin knew, from the fourth and fifth year, boys
with braying laughs and sudden, falsetto giggles, boys who
stood on street corners and watched girls walk past, who
punched each other with painful tenderness, who cultivated
small moustaches that broke down, when shaved, into crusts
of acne thicker than the moustaches had ever been, who lit
cigarettes behind cupped hands, narrowing their eyes in
pretended indifference to the smoke.

Colin worshipped from a safe distance, too wary to approach
on his own. But then his friend Ross came running up, and
together they walked boldly up the steps.

At the top, in a glass display case, was a poster advertising that week's film. A man in flying helmet and goggles straddled the scene. Between his legs, blazing planes plunged out of the sky, men in parachutes floated down. Underneath the billowing white, their bodies looked soft and squishy, like moths.

Ross nudged Colin. 'C'mon.'

'Fifteen,' said the woman in the ticket-booth.

'What?' said Ross. 'Aw, *howay*.'

'Fifteen.'

Ross stood on tiptoe to look her more convincingly in the eye. 'We are fifteen.'

'Pull the other one, love. It's got bells on.'

"S *true*.' Ross leaned forward, confidentially. 'It's the fags, Miss. They don't half stunt your growth.'

'What you on, son? Five hundred a day? Go on, hop it, before I fetch the manager.'

They left. Drifted across the road in silence, and in silence sat down on the kerb. Groups of people walked up the steps of the cinema, laughing and chattering, certain of getting in.

'There's *Son of Paleface* on at the Gaumont,' said Ross. 'Roy Rogers.'

'Bugger Roy Rogers.'

They sat in silence, watching the people go in.

'I suppose we could . . .'

But Colin didn't get a chance to finish.

'There's our Mick!' said Ross.

Before Colin could react Ross was on his feet and running. A car braked hard to avoid him. The driver wound down the window, and shouted, but Ross had already reached the other side. By the time Colin got there, he was well launched on his plea. 'Aw, go on,' he was saying. 'All you have to do is nip round the back. They'll think you've gone for a pee.'

Mick hesitated.

'And even if we did get caught we wouldn't crack on who did it. Go on.'

Mick's girlfriend came down the steps to see what was happening. She was wearing a blue-and-white polka-dot dress, with white shoes and a white handbag, and her petticoats crackled when she moved. Angie Dixon.

'Howay, Mick,' she said. 'It'll've started.'

'Coming.' Mick turned to Ross. 'All right, but no sitting with us, mind.'

'Don't worry, you'll get your snog.'

'And you'll get a clip round the lughole.'

Mick took the girl's arm and they went up the steps together.

'What was all that about?' Colin asked.

'He's gunna open the fire-door for us. C'mon.'

Ross hauled Colin round the corner into the side-street, where he leant against the metal door, pretending to be interested in a row that was developing outside Brown's fish shop. Colin went and stood beside him, listening for Mick's footsteps on the other side of the door, but for a long time nothing happened. Momentarily, Colin closed his eyes.

Rifle-fire cracked out. A man threw up his arms, caught like a runner breasting the tape, and held for a moment, before he slowly fell.

'Here we go.'

The fire-door clanged open, and Colin felt himself dragged inside.

'You aren't half slow,' Ross said, bitterly.

A corridor with dirty beige walls and a stone floor stretched out in front of them.

'This way,' whispered Ross.

Colin pushed the door open and began to follow Mick, whom he could just see at the bottom of one of the aisles, but Ross pulled him back. They stood with their backs against the wall until their eyes became accustomed to the blue-grey light.

'Look for a married couple,' Ross whispered. 'They'll think we're with them.'

They waited till a crescendo of rifle-fire pinned everybody's attention to the screen, then tiptoed down the aisle. Ross had spotted a middle-aged couple with two vacant seats beside them. They crept into these seats, and fixed their eyes on the screen.

A man was standing at the top of a high tower with hundreds of people looking up at him, waiting for him to jump. Beads of sweat gathered on his upper lip. As he looked down, he swayed, and the ground beneath him blurred.

The man standing behind him – an instructor of some sort – said, 'Go on'. And then you saw his feet, sticking out over the edge of the platform, and the sheer drop beneath.

He leapt. The parachute flowered. He drifted down, landing safely. You saw him bundle the cloth together, and then the other men came crowding round, puzzled because he'd taken so long. Nobody knew he was afraid.

Then he was in bed, awake, and the sweat was back on his lip. The camera moved in close, until you were looking at one eye, and in the pupil of that eye a shape formed, the shape of a parachute that didn't open, but fluttered endlessly towards the ground.

Next day came the first real jump. The first man to go looked nervous, standing by the open door. He didn't seem to jump. It was almost as if the wind plucked him from the plane. Everybody craned forward, expecting the routine billowing of white, but nothing happened, only a brief, endless fluttering, and the thud of something heavy hitting the ground.

The camera zoomed in on the face of the frightened man, and you saw his terror.

After that the story speeded up. The men were parachuted behind enemy lines to blow up an ammunition dump, but Colin was scarcely aware of the bursting bombs, the screams of burned and dying men. Again and again, he saw the man dangling from his harness, as the parachute hurtled towards the ground. When Ross nudged him, he jumped.

'C'mon,' Ross said, 'we'd better get going.'

The audience was already on its feet, some of them running up the aisles in their determination to avoid 'God Save The Queen'. Here and there an elderly couple, or a young man in uniform, stood to attention. Under cover of the crowd, Colin and Ross slipped out on to the street.

'Good, wasn't it?' said Ross.

'Yeh,' Colin said, but he had to force the enthusiasm into his voice. He hadn't liked the frightened man.

Once, a couple of years ago, Viv had talked to him about his father. She'd described how, one night, she and her friend had waited outside the aerodrome, but only her friend's boyfriend came striding across the tarmac to meet them. Colin's father had been killed in a bombing raid the night before. Viv, not wanting to spoil her friend's pleasure, had walked home, alone.

It was a moving story, the way Viv told it. Colin was moved. He was moved again a few nights later when he saw the same story on the screen of the Gaumont. A plane exploded, violins swelled, tears glistened, a young girl walked home, alone.

He'd never believed anything Viv said since.

'She made it up,' he told his nan afterwards.

'I wouldn't be too sure of that. Your mam sounds like the pictures even when she's telling the truth.'

For Colin, the mystery of his father's identity was bound up with the war, the war he'd been born into, but couldn't remember. The war whose relics he saw around him everywhere. Photographs. On mantelpieces, in friends' houses, dads with more hair than they had now sat astride guns, or smiled against the backdrop of ruined cities. A little coaxing, and they'd show you the things they'd brought back. Guns, knives, a swastika ring, gold teeth sawn from a Japanese corpse.

At school, too, the endless war between British and Germans was re-fought at every break, and the leaders of the opposing armies were always boys whose fathers had been in the war. Who could produce, when need arose, the ultimate authority: *My dad says.*

Everything *Colin* knew about the war came from films. Perhaps that was why he hadn't liked the film tonight. He didn't want to be told about men being frightened. He wanted to be told about heroes.

Ross nudged his arm. 'You going straight home?'

'Suppose so.'

They cut up the steps to the town centre, and began walking along the main shopping street.

'Hey,' Ross said suddenly, and pointed.

'What?' said Colin.

'See that?'

Colin looked more closely. Blond hair, piled high, a black dress with lace round the collar.

'Yes?'

'That's a fella.'

Colin looked again, expecting to see a man standing behind the woman. But no. Ross must mean her.

'It never is.'

'It bloody is, you know.'

'Her? You need your eyes seeing to.'

'It's not a her. It's a him.'

Colin stopped. 'You're having me on.'

'No, I'm not. If you don't believe me go and have a look.'

'No.' Colin walked on a few steps.

'Go on.'

'What am I supposed to say? "Good evening, Madam, me friend says you're a man"?'

'*No.* Ask him the time. Go on.'

Colin went across. It isn't true, he thought. And the closer he got the more sure he was that it couldn't be true, because she'd got nylons on, high heels, everything. He couldn't see her face because she'd turned round to look in the shop window.

Colin looked too, scuffing the sleeve of his jumper along the glass. The models were naked, wrapped in brown paper so you couldn't see what they'd got. Once, he'd lain on the floor, getting chewing gum stuck to the back of his blazer, and his reward had been the glimpse of a smooth, hairless, ungrooved mound. The models had looked down on him with cool, amused, supercilious eyes.

Colin took a deep breath. 'Excuse me, Miss. Have you got the time?'

The face that turned towards him was heavily made up. A shiny cupid's bow had been painted over a thin mouth, and the lipstick had leaked into the creases of the upper lip. As Colin stared, the lips opened, and a deep, baritone voice said, 'Piss off, sonny.'

Colin ran. On the other side of the road Ross was bent double. 'It's Bernie Walters,' he said. 'You know, he keeps the sweetshop.'

'Why does he do it?'

'How should I know?' Ross looked at Colin, curiously. 'He just does.'

Colin stared behind him, seeing again the shiny, red mouth and the man's voice that had come out of it. He didn't speak again, until they parted at the corner of Ross's street.

'See you tomorrow night,' Ross said.

'Yeh.'

He was hardly aware of Ross leaving. He began walking automatically in the direction of his own home, along Ross's street and into Clifford Avenue. Here, all the trees had white bands painted round their trunks. For a long time Colin hadn't known why, but then Viv said it was because of the blackout. Before the trees were marked, people used to bump into them and hurt themselves.

When he was nine Colin used to zigzag from pavement to pavement, touching every band on every tree. He couldn't have walked past a tree without touching it. Now, of course, he realized that was childish, and yet, as he walked past first one tree and then another, his fear grew. He felt the trees close in behind him as he passed, but he didn't dare look round.

He began to hurry. It was too early to go home, he thought. At the end of Clifford Avenue, he turned right, and headed back into town.

5

Crowds of people poured down the narrow steps that led from the upper part of the town, with its hotels and boarding houses, to the seafront, a crammed half mile of cafés, pubs, gift shops and amusement arcades.

A gang of youths and girls swept along the pavement, arms linked, singing as they came – sweat, Brylcreem, beer, Evening in Paris – and then they were gone, and the sound of their singing, fading in the distance, left Colin feeling smaller, shivery and alone.

For want of anything better to do he drifted in under the glittering golden arch of the fun-fair, and began to wander around. Shouts, screams, the grind and rattle of the dodgems, red, green, blue, orange lights flashing – the heat and noise overwhelmed him, and for a moment he rested with his back against the guard rail of the Ferris wheel.

At the goldfish stall, near by, a man had just succeeded in getting a ping-pong ball into one of the bowls, and was trying to persuade his small son that he'd really like a big, pink teddy bear to take home with him rather than a goldfish.

The little boy howled, batting the teddy bear away with his clenched fist.

'We've nowhere to keep a fish in the van,' said his father. 'And even if we had how the bloody hell are we going to get it back on the train?'

'Da-ad!'

The stall-keeper, a blonde woman with brawny arms, waited, impassive, a pink teddy bear in one hand, a green fishing net in the other.

'We could put it in a jam jar,' the boy's mother said.

'That's right, give in to him. It's you giving in to him that's got him the way he is.'

The blonde woman caught a fish, and put it in a small jar.

'Here, I'll take that,' the mother said.

'No,' the child said.

Tight-lipped, the father hoisted his son on to his shoulders, grasping the thin legs in the palms of both huge hands.

Hiccuping in triumph over his dying prize, the boy was borne away, high above the shoulders of the crowd, while mother trudged along behind, clutching a green vase won at another stall, and three woolly cardigans brought along just in case.

THE RAILWAY STATION

A man lies dead. Face downward, arms outstretched, just as he fell. Cautiously, the guards approach.

Von Strohm kicks his side, then gestures to the guards who heave him over onto his back.

Wide open eyes stare unseeing at the roof.

VON STROHM

See what I mean? Lift a stone up, anywhere in this bloody country, and half a dozen of them crawl out.

He's talking to a much younger man who stands deferentially beside him.

Random identity checks. That's what gets them. Every time.

He turns to the guards.

Let's have the suitcase open. And get rid of that lot!

He waves his arm towards the railings that divide the platform from the rest of the station.

Staring through the railings are people previously seen in the queue. They show no emotion, but the blankness of their faces is threatening. Unexpectedly, they begin to chant:

FRENCH CIVILIANS

All the twos, twenty-two. Kelly's eye . . .

. . . number one. Two fat ladies, eighty-eight. On its own, number nine . . .'

Colin walked along behind the row of mainly middle-aged or elderly women, each hunched over her card, a beer-bottle top poised for the next number.

'Never been kissed, one and . . .'

'House!'

A buzz of excitement, the clink of bottle-tops as cards were cleared, and then a white-haired, old lady shouted out, 'Never mind never been kissed, I think you want your balls shook up!'

The housey-housey teller, a fair-haired young man with a cold in his nose, started to blush, and a ripple of amusement spread along the row.

Colin went to the booth at the centre of the amusement arcade, and got change for half a crown. A stout, middle-aged woman leant against the wall of the booth, perhaps waiting for a vacant place at the housey table. She carried a canvas bag with a thermos flask sticking out, and her stockings were powdered white where the Blanco from her sandals had rubbed off.

'By, it's hot, isn't it, son?' she said, wiping her forehead with the back of a meaty hand. 'I'm roasted.'

A man, wearing a dark suit with a waistcoat and watch-chain came to join her. 'You all right now?' she asked.

'I've made room for more.'

'Aye, it's all right for some. You want to see the Ladies. They're queuing right round the block.'

'You could go on the beach.'

'I could not!'

'Why not? I'd keep a look-out.'

'Aye, I know what you'd be looking at.'

They moved off, still arguing. A few yards further on, Colin heard: 'We are *married*, Ethel.'

Colin slipped away and for the next few minutes shot ball bearings up sloping tables whose flashing lights showed astro-nomical scores. Music from the juke-box pounded through his skull and, at intervals, the policeman in the glass case by the door clutched his fat sides and gave vent to bursts of mechan-ical laughter. 'Ho, ho, ho, ho,' roared the policeman, rubber cheeks bulging as he swayed. 'Ho, ho, ho, ho.'

The laughter, repeated every few minutes, echoed round and round the arcade.

Colin paid a penny and watched a man hang, a clockwork execution, complete with jerks on the end of the rope. He was reminded, as he watched, of the frightened man and the parachute that failed to open, but this would be worse, he thought, because you would stand there, on the trap door, and you would *know* you were going to die.

Next to him two boys sniggered over 'My Lady's Toilet', but they were a lot older than Colin. You were supposed to be twenty-one before you watched that. Colin had never dared, though he and Ross had often lingered by the machine, Ross always pointing to the word 'toilet' and giggling, though Colin kept telling him it didn't mean that.

He waited till the boys were gone, then slipped a penny in the slot. He didn't know what gave him the courage, except that the policeman's repeated bursts of laughter had set his teeth on edge.

'My Lady' turned out to be a plump, rather motherly woman, who sensibly kept her vest on much of the time. She smiled, a little shyly, Colin thought, as if aware of being watched. He tried to convince himself he was excited, even pressing his cock furtively against the edge of the machine, but he wasn't, not really. Her corsets were exactly like his nan's.

A slap of flesh on metal, and there, on either side of him, were a man's arms, bare to the elbow, covered in fair hairs. Colin's heart bulged. He turned, expecting to see the manager.

'Adrian. You didn't half give me a shock.'

'Mucky little bugger, you want shocking. Here, move over, let's have a look.'

Colin watched him, noticing how the brown skin became abruptly white just inside the rolled up sleeves of his shirt.

'Don't think much of that,' Adrian said, raising his head. 'You can't see nowt. You been on the hanging one?'

'Yeh.'

'That's Crippen, that is. The bloke in there.'

Colin looked again at the machine. He hadn't known the story was true, that the man who fell through the trap door had been real, like Derek Bentley and Ruth Ellis had been real.

'What the fuck is going on here?' Brian Combey was leaning against one of the pillars. 'I thought you were just behind me.'

'I bumped into the kid.'

Adrian sounded apologetic, almost nervous, Colin thought. Nothing like he sounded at home.

Colin had never been so close to Brian Combey before. He saw the oily skin that seemed to have heat trapped inside it, like tar on roads at the end of a hot day. He would have liked to back away, but was afraid of drawing attention to himself. He needn't have worried. Combey's eyes flicked over him, and passed on.

'Are we going to the frigging pub, or aren't we?'

'Yeah.'

Colin hated seeing Adrian jump to obey.

'Apart from anything else that bloody copper's getting on me nerves.' He turned to Colin, as the policeman's metallic laugh rang out again, and unexpectedly smiled. 'There's nowt worse than a happy policeman.'

Kneeling on the station platform, von Strohm is not so much happy as ecstatic. His young assistant has smashed the lock on the suitcase, and opened it to reveal, as expected, a wireless and headphones.

VON STROHM

Go on, lift it out.

His glee fades as the space underneath is seen to be empty.

Try the lining.

The assistant produces a knife and slashes the thin silk.

There has to be a codebook. The wireless is useless without it.

ASSISTANT

Well, it's not here. And it's not in any of his pockets.

VON STROHM

Then somebody else on the train must have had it. He wouldn't travel without it.

ASSISTANT

Perhaps we should've cordoned off the area? Searched everybody.

VON STROHM

It isn't important. I can remember every face in the queue.

His eyes narrow. Clearly, he's remembering one face in particular.

I can pick him up whenever I want.

Colin sat on the sea wall, watching the stream of people, heads bobbing, move up and down the front. The pavements were gritty with sand, the night air flashed red, blue, green, orange, and the cars crawled along, their bumpers nudging the backs of sun-reddened legs.

Behind him, a wave creamed over and withdrew, seething among the pebbles.

Urged along by the soldiers' rifle-butts, the French civilians disperse.

Gaston is met by a middle-aged man, Pierre. A gingery moustache, the beginnings of a paunch, cow eyes, but under all this an impression of strength.

Their meeting is observed by a man in black, who's leaning against one of the pillars, unmolested by the guards. He lowers his newspaper, and gets ready to follow them.

PIERRE

If only he'd kept his nerve.

He'd been out here six months. It's a long time.

They weren't even looking for you.

Who were they looking for?

A bridge got blown up a few days back. They've been doing random checks ever since.

As they leave the station, the man in black detaches himself from the shadows, and starts to follow them down the hill into the town.

Were you seen together? Did you sit together on the train?

Of course not.

We'll have to get a message to Maurice. He'll have to warn London they've got the code book.

Have they?

Pierre stares at him. Gaston taps his jacket.

And you walked through the barrier with that?

There wasn't a lot of choice.

You must burn it the minute we get back.

Don't worry. I wasn't thinking of walking round the town with it.

He looks over his shoulder, made momentarily uneasy by the man in black, who follows at a steady pace. Gaston watches for a while, then turns back to Pierre.

GASTON

They're on to us now.

PIERRE
(*shakes his head*)

The poor devil's dead — he can't tell them anything. They don't know any more now than they did before.

GASTON

They know there's something *to* know. With the Gestapo that's enough.

Brakes squealed, Colin felt himself hauled back. He stood, gasping, in the grip of somebody he couldn't see.

A woman, her face looming towards him like a reflection in the back of a spoon, said, 'Are you all right, son?' Powder clung to the fine down on her upper lip.

The grip on his arm relaxed.

Somewhere to the side, a man's voice, harsher. 'You want to watch where you're going, son. If that bloke there hadn't grabbed you, you'd've been under that car.'

Dazed, wanting only to get away from the gaping faces, Colin staggered across the road. Only when he'd reached the other side, did he realize he hadn't thanked the man who'd saved him. He turned, meaning to go back, and stopped.

For there, impossibly, on the other side of the road, stood

the man in black, the man who'd followed Gaston and Pierre down the hill from the railway station.

He stared at Colin for a full minute, then turned rapidly on his heel and strode away.

6

Colin stopped outside Mrs Hennigan's flat. She was watching television, but looked up when she heard the front door open.

'What was the picture like, pet?'

'OK.'

Colin knew Mrs Hennigan was often lonely so he felt he had to stay and talk, though he didn't want to. He wanted to go upstairs and think about the man in black. He could see him now, as tall and thin and dark as an exclamation mark, against the hurrying crowds.

Mrs Hennigan came to the living-room door. 'Be a war picture, was it, son?'

'Yeh.'

'Beats me what people see in them.'

'It was packed.'

'Oh, it would be, I believe you. I still don't know what people see in it. It was bad enough having to live through it, without raking it up again every week.'

Probably she didn't want to be reminded of Adrian's father, who'd been killed in the war. *Really* killed, Colin thought. Unlike his own.

Mrs Hennigan seemed to hesitate. 'I don't suppose you bumped into our Adrian on your travels, did you?'

'No,' Colin said. He searched for something else to say. 'I saw Mick.'

'Oh aye? He'd be with his girlfriend, was he?'

'Yeh. At the pictures.'

'Angie Dixon. Nice lass. I just wish our Adrian could get on with somebody like that.'

'He's had plenty of girlfriends.'

'Ah, but it never seems to come to anything, does it? He's never once walked a girl through that door and said, Mam, this is . . .' She waved her hand. 'I wouldn't care who it was, long as she was a nice lass and thought a bit about him.'

Behind her, on the screen, a woman in a strapless evening dress stopped talking, and smiled. The picture faded. A few seconds later the Queen, also smiling, appeared. She was on horseback, taking the salute at the trooping of the colour.

'Oh, well,' said Mrs Hennigan. 'That's that for the night. Do you know, some of the turns I've seen on there tonight, they'd've been hissed off the stage at the music hall.' She'd grumbled about the television set ever since Coronation day, but she never switched it off.

'I think I'd better be getting to bed,' Colin said.

'Aye, son, up you go.' She watched him up the first flight of stairs. 'Don't you be frightened now. Remember I'm just down here.'

Colin never got to sleep before Viv came in. He was too afraid of the dark, afraid of how it pressed against the glass of windows, and seeped through the cracks in floorboards and walls. He left the lamp on and the curtains open. Moths, fat, pale moths, fumbled the pane.

He got into bed and pulled the bedclothes up around his ears. He was afraid that when he tried to sleep he would see the man in black, but he needn't have worried. The moment he closed his eyes, Bernie's face appeared. Blue eyelids, lashes gobby with mascara, the mouth red, shockingly red, Colin remembered, like a horse's arsehole just before it shits.

He opened his eyes again, wondering why it should be Bernie's face he saw.

THE CAFÉ

Evening. The bar is crowded, mainly with off-duty German soldiers, though a few tables are occupied by Frenchmen.

Two waitresses, Vivienne and Paulette, move between the tables, serving the drinks. In the far corner an old man is playing the piano.

Pierre is looking into the mirror that lines the wall behind the bar. A flaw distorts his reflection. He bobs from side to side, making his forehead first bulge and then recede. An oddly childish game for a middle-aged man.

Gaston comes up behind him. Gaston is British, twelve years old, parachuted into France because of his superb command of the French language.

PIERRE

Ah, Gaston!

Mon oncle!

Silence. Pierre glances round the bar.

PIERRE

Have you burnt the codebook?

GASTON

Yes.

He nudges Pierre, indicating the darkest corner where the man in black sits, alone.

Who is he?

Pierre peers into the corner, but clearly can't see the man's face. He shrugs.

PIERRE

I don't know. I've never seen him before. He can't be one of their agents. We know all of them.

They wait. Gaston wipes the counter, Pierre polishes a wine glass, and holds it up to the light.
Distorted by the curve of the glass, a woman enters, heavily made up, and alone. She looks round, nervously licking her dark red lips.

PIERRE

That's him.

GASTON

Impossible!

PIERRE

That's Bernard. I told you he was a master of disguise.

Gaston, still unconvinced, picks up a tray and goes across to the table. He stares at the backs of the woman's — suspiciously broad — hands.

BERNARD
(*A throaty contralto*)
Quickly! There's no time.

Military vehicles can be heard drawing up outside the door. A shout of command. The crunch of boots on gravel.

Drop something!

With his customary speed of reaction, Gaston drops the tray. As he bends to pick it up, Bernard slides a thin package inside his shirt. Simultaneously, a squad of German soldiers bursts into the café, followed by von Strohm.

The piano tinkles into silence. One by one, and then in a rush, the off-duty soldiers struggle to their feet.

Von Strohm looks around, noting Gaston, noting the man in black, though his eyes come finally to rest on Bernard.

VON STROHM
That one.

Bernard is dragged, protesting in the same feminine voice, to the door. He does not look at Gaston or Pierre. With a final glare von Strohm goes.

The German soldiers sit down again. A buzz of conversation springs up immediately at their tables, but the French are slower to recover.

Paulette crosses to the piano and persuades the old man to start playing again. She looks across at Gaston who nods his head approvingly. Casually, he strolls back to the bar.

PIERRE
Did you get the plans?

GASTON
Yes.

PIERRE
Not that they'll be any use to us now.

GASTON

What do you mean?

PIERRE

How long do you suppose it'll be before Bernard talks? A day?
Two days?

GASTON

He won't talk.

PIERRE

Of course he'll talk. Even the bravest talk in the end.

GASTON

Not Bernard.

PIERRE

Oh, yes, my young friend, even Bernard.

*Gaston looks across the café. He meets the gaze of the man in black,
whose deeply shadowed eyes seem to hold the glint of mysterious
knowledge.*

A car's headlamps trailed curtains of light across the ceiling.
Colin threw back the bedclothes and ran to the window. Viv
was just getting out of the car. She bent down to talk to the
driver, shifting her weight from one foot to the other, hugging
herself in the cold wind that blew along the street.

Colin could just see the driver's face, leaning across and
looking up. It was Reg Boyce, the manager of the nightclub
where Viv worked. Viv had brought him home once, on her
evening off, and he'd laughed a lot and called Colin 'Sonny
Jim'. Viv bent and kissed him. Colin watched, his face orange
in the light of the street-lamp beneath his window.

Then, just as Colin was expecting the car to drive away, Mr

Boyce got out and slammed the door on his side. She was bringing him in.

In his bedroom above the café, Gaston watches the street.

Beneath the window, a car draws up with a scarlet-and-black flag on its bonnet. Vivienne, accompanied by a German officer, gets out . . .

Gaston turns from the window. Pierre is immediately behind him, and other men are ranged around the walls. In silence they listen to footsteps, and Vivienne's muffled laughter, coming up the stairs.

GASTON
(*quietly*)
We can't let this go on, Pierre. It's far too dangerous.

PIERRE
She's no traitor, Gaston. In fact once or twice she's given us valuable information.

GASTON
And how much has gone the other way? It's no good, Pierre. She's got to go.

PIERRE
You mean, sack her?

GASTON
No, Pierre. I don't mean sack her.

Pierre looks at Gaston, then at the other men. Their faces are hard, accusing, without mercy.

In the next room, the bedsprings had started to creak. Colin closed his eyes, and pictures from 'My Lady's Toilet', mixed with Viv's face, and Bernie's face, jumbled together in his mind. Crippen jerked at the end of a rope, von Strohm gazed along the station platform, once again the young man ran and died.

After a while the creaking stopped, but still Colin couldn't get to sleep. He got out of bed, crossed to the window, and looked down into the street, where he saw what seemed to be a figure in a black coat looking up at him. He stepped back and let the curtain fall.

His arm ached, in five distinct places, like a grip still tightening.

Friday

7

Colin knew he was being followed as soon as he left the house. At the end of the road, he stopped, and pretended to look in a shop window. Out of the corner of his eye he saw the man slow down and stop too.

For a moment he was tempted to go back, to say he felt too ill for school. It wouldn't be much of a lie, anyway, he did feel ill. Shivery.

He walked on again, but slowly, feeling exposed and vulnerable, as if a layer of skin had been stripped from his back. He wanted to run, but then if the man ran too it would confirm what Colin already knew, and he wasn't ready to have it confirmed.

For perhaps the first time in his life, Colin passed through the school gates with a sense of relief. He didn't bother looking back. He knew the man couldn't follow him into the playground.

Several teachers had already started the registers. He ran along beneath the high, meshed windows, waiting for Mr Sedgewick's voice.

'Abbott?'

'Present, Sir.'

'Adamson?'

'Sir.'

'Blake?'

'Here, Sir.'

Through the swing doors, and along the bottom corridor. The walls were lined with photographs of football teams.

'Booth?'

'Sir.'

'Carmichael?'

'Present, Sir.'

'Dodds?'

'Sir.'

Nearly there. And then, suddenly, a prefect.

'You couldn't *conceivably* have been *running*, could you, Harper?'

An affected drawl. Colin wondered who Roberts was trying to be.

'No, Roberts.'

'*Good*. I'm glad you weren't, because if you had been I *might* have had to put you in detention.'

Sensing that Roberts had turned to stare after him, Colin forced himself to walk the rest of the way.

'Evans?'

'Present, Sir.'

'Harper?'

Silence.

'Harper?' Then, increasingly impatient, 'Has anybody seen Harper?'

Colin pushed open the door and walked in.

'Ah, Harper. You come most carefully upon your cue.' Mr Sedgewick stopped smiling. 'Why are you late? Or perhaps I should say, Why are you late, *this time*?'

Colin hesitated. 'I'm not late, Sir. You haven't finished marking the register.'

'Harper, you are supposed to be in this school at five to nine. It is now . . .' An elaborate, unnecessary consultation of the watch. '*Five past* nine. You are late, Harper. *Present*, but *late*.'

'Slept in, Sir.'

'Well, that excuse certainly has the benefit of being well-tried. As I recall you slept in yesterday, and the day before, and the day before that.'

'Yes, Sir.'

'I don't think I can be bothered to speak to you, Harper. Sit down.'

Colin turned to go to his seat.

'And of course you will do *yet another* detention tonight.'

'Half an hour, Sir?'

'No, Harper. An *hour*. If you sit on your bottom long enough you might just possibly learn the value of time.'

Colin sat near the back. A hot-water pipe with the paint flaking from it ran along beside his desk, gurgling at intervals. There was a smell of warm dust.

Mr Sedgewick continued with the register and then dealt with the sick-notes. Colin sat with his arms folded and wondered why he was always in trouble. It wasn't just being late. It was not getting his report signed, not wearing a tie . . . Everything.

As if reading his mind, Mr Sedgewick, shielding his eyes with his hand, said, 'Harper, I hardly dare mention this. Have you brought your report?'

'Yes, Sir.'

'And is it signed?'

'Yes, Sir.'

'I am *amazed*.'

He held out his hand to take the report, like a robot, face averted. Colin went out to the front to give it to him. Mr Sedgewick brought it closer to his face in stages, scanning it quickly. Colin could see him trying to think of something disparaging to say, but there wasn't a lot that could be said. That was what infuriated them most: his work was good.

'Well,' said Mr Sedgewick. 'That's one little drama over then. Until next term.'

Colin began to edge away.

'Harper, are you wearing a tie?'

Despite the weather, Colin was wearing a thick, winter pullover, with a high neck. He'd been wearing it all week, and so far nobody had noticed the missing tie. 'No, Sir.'

'May one ask why not?'

Colin felt the other boys staring at him, enjoying the break in routine. 'I haven't got one, Sir.'

'What do you mean, you haven't got one?'

'I've lost it, Sir.'

A pause. 'You've checked lost property?'

'Yes, Sir. Several times, Sir.'

'Well then, your mother'll just have to buy you a new one, won't she? It is your mother, isn't it?'

Colin opened his mouth, and stopped.

'Well?'

'I've asked her, Sir. She says she's got better things to spend her money on.'

'Like floppy ears and a cottonwool tail, I suppose?'

You could hear the intake of breath.

Colin waited, then: 'Enjoy your night out, did you, Sir?'

Mr Sedgewick began to bluster, spraying the front row with spit as he always did when something really got under his skin. 'I'm afraid I can't let this go,' he said. 'You'll have to go and see Mr Sawdon after Assembly.'

The bell rang. Immediately, the boys clattered to their feet.

'How many times? How many times do I have to say it? *The bell is for me*. The bell is to tell *me* the time. It has absolutely nothing whatsoever to do with you.'

Slowly, one by one, the boys sat down again. Outside, other classes had begun to walk past on their way to Assembly.

'When I say the word, you will get up, put your chairs under your desks, *quietly*, line up *quietly* by the door – QUIETLY – and then – once again *when I give the word* – you will walk down the corridor. What do I mean when I say walk?'

Most of the class looked puzzled. Then a few hands inched upwards.

'Jenkins?'

'You mean WALK, Sir?'

'That's right.'

Another painful silence. Outside, the stream of footsteps had become a trickle.

'I am giving the word . . .' Mr Sedgewick raised his hand. 'NOW.'

The hall was taller than the classroom, its ceiling vaulted. A large window, with a design of eagles in stained glass, filled most of the far wall. Immediately beneath it stood a small stage, with a lectern, and a row of chairs behind, where the teachers sat. The body of the hall was full of folding chairs, most of them already occupied.

Mr Sedgewick appeared on the platform, as Colin's class filed into the two rows of empty seats. Finally, when the hall was silent – even the sporadic coughing had stopped – a tall, thin figure, wearing a gown and mortarboard, strode through the ranks of standing boys and mounted the platform.

Mr Sawdon gazed from side to side. It seemed impossible that the silence should deepen, but it did.

'Good morning, school.'

A murmur of response, totally unlike the well-drilled, mechanical quacking Colin remembered from junior school.

The hall was packed: fair, black, brown, auburn heads all facing the same way. Here and there, a shaft of light, falling through the stained-glass eagles, turned a hand or the side of a face to gold.

'Hymn number 172.'

The hymn was sung; the boys sat down. A tall, spindly sixth-former stepped forward to read the lesson, gabbling the words to get through it as fast as possible. He managed fairly well, until he came to a whole string of 'whatsoevers' and there he ground to a halt. At last, though, he was able to step back, his blush fading to leave the skin a greasy white.

'Let us pray.'

During prayers, Colin read the honours boards. Most recorded the names and dates of boys who'd gone on to university and got degrees, but three were lists of boys killed in one or other of the two world wars. Colin was trying to work out how many names appeared on both lists, when he happened to glance towards the platform, and found Mr Sedgewick watching him. Hastily, he bowed his head.

Mr Sawdon's prayers, like Pond's lipstick, went on and on and on. Colin, forced to keep his eyes shut, passed the time trying to imagine what Mr Sedgewick would be like in bed.

'Mildred, what do I mean when I say fuck?'

'Oh, Cedric,' gasped Mildred, her long, scarlet fingernails plucking at the knot of his pyjama cord, 'You mean FUCK.'

A ripple of amusement. Colin opened his eyes in surprise. It wasn't all that funny.

High above him, on the dais, Mr Sawdon said, not unkindly, 'The rest of us are sitting down.'

Colin stared around at the rows and rows of boys, at the

eyes, and the mouths opening to swallow him. He sank into his chair, causing another ripple of laughter, and prayed, more fervently than he'd ever prayed in his life, for the roof to fall in and cover him.

8

'You've been late three times in one week,' Mr Sawdon said. 'Not good enough, is it?'

'No, Sir.'

It wasn't three times, it was four, but Colin didn't feel obliged to point that out.

'So what are we going to do about it. *Eh*?'

'I don't know, Sir.'

Mr Sawdon sighed. 'Sit down, Harper.'

Colin sat down. Mr Sawdon came and sat opposite, on the other side of the desk. The branches of the tree outside his window were momentarily reflected in his glasses, so that he looked blind.

'*Why* were you late? *Eh*?'

'I slept in, Sir.'

'Well, yes, I'm sure you did, but then the question is still: *Why*?' He leant back in his chair. 'What time did you go to bed?'

Colin stared at Mr Sawdon across wider divisions than the desk, wondering at what time, in Mr Sawdon's world, twelve-year-old boys went to bed. 'Nine o'clock, Sir?'

Mr Sawdon didn't reply. He'd made a steeple with his fingertips, alternately pressing them together and bouncing them apart. At last he said, 'So how do you account for the fact that I saw you walking along Clifford Avenue at half past ten?'

Oh, *sod*.

'I'd been to see a friend, Sir.' He looked down to avoid Mr Sawdon's gaze. 'I meant nine as a general rule.'

'Well, no wonder you slept in. You can't have been in bed before . . . eleven?'

'No, Sir.'

A long silence. Then Mr Sawdon leant forward, clasping his hands together on the blotting pad. 'I believe your father's . . .'

'Dead, Sir.'

Colin stared at Mr Sawdon's hands, and concentrated on looking stricken. He knew he did it well. He also knew if you did it well enough, it shut people up.

Mr Sawdon hesitated. 'The war?'

'Yes, Sir.' Colin understood, perhaps for the first time, why his mother lied about his father. People did not have an automatic right to know. 'I don't remember him, Sir. It was before I was born.'

'And your mother's a waitress?'

'Yes, Sir.'

Mr Sawdon examined his fingernails. 'In a nightclub?'

Colin said again, more cautiously, 'Yes, Sir.'

Abruptly Mr Sawdon got to his feet and began pacing up and down behind Colin's chair. 'She must get back from work rather late?'

'Yes, Sir.' Colin didn't like the way things were going. 'I'm not left on me own, Sir. Mrs Hennigan's always there.'

Bernard faces the empty chair of his interrogator, von Strohm, who paces up and down behind him.

VON STROHM

Why do you insist on holding out in this ridiculous way? Nobody's going to rescue you. They don't even know where you are. You could make things so much easier for yourself, Bernard, if only you'd be reasonable.

He bends over Bernard, his hands appearing suddenly on the arms of the chair.

For example, that girl, the waitress. What's her name? Vivienne. Is she one of you?

BERNARD

One of who? You talk in riddles, my friend.

VON STROHM

Your group, your cell, whatever you call it. The Resistance.

Bernard tries to speak, but von Strohm interrupts.

She has many friends among German officers. In fact only yesterday evening she was seen returning to her apartment in the company of the Kommandant. (*Pauses*) We need to know a lot more about her.

BERNARD

Then you'd better ask the Kommandant. As far as I know, she's just a waitress.

VON STROHM
(*in Mrs Hinde's prissiest voice*)
Not what they called it in our young day.

Von Strohm claps his hand to his mouth, momentarily disconcerted, but Bernard appears to notice nothing.

BERNARD
I don't go into that café very often. It was only accident I was there last night.

VON STROHM
(*smiles*)
Save yourself, Bernard. After all, nobody's ever going to know what happened in this room.

His expression hardens.

Either way.

'You've been in this school, how long . . . ?'
He knew that as well as Colin did. 'Just over a year, Sir.'
'Do you like it here? *Eh?*'
'I suppose so, Sir.'
'You suppose?'
Colin didn't know what to say.
'Do you know when this school was founded?'
'1588, Sir.'
The same year as the . . . ?'
'Defeat of the Spanish Armada, Sir.'
Colin couldn't see that this had anything to do with whether he liked the school, but he could see Mr Sawdon thought it had.
'Have you made any particular friends at school?'
'No, Sir.'
'So whom do you play with after school?'

Colin shrugged. 'Lads I know, Sir.'

'I see. You mean boys from the Secondary Modern school?'

'Yes, Sir.'

'I don't suppose they get very much homework, do they?'

'No, Sir.'

'Isn't that a bit difficult? I mean, when they want to go out, and you have to stay in.'

All Colin's homework was done at break in the cloakroom at school, but he could scarcely tell Mr Sawdon that. 'Is a bit, Sir.'

'Wouldn't it be better – *easier* – if you spent more time with boys from *this* school? *Eh*?'

Colin stared at his clasped hands.

'You see, Harper, it does seem to me that sooner or later you're going to have to make up your mind whether you belong to this school, or not.'

He waited.

'Yes, Sir.'

'Now, I don't want to be too harsh on this occasion because I can see that in some ways life must be quite . . . difficult. It's not easy for a boy, growing up without a father. But I will say this. If you would join in with some of the extracurricular activities we have in the school, you would find it an enriching experience. But even more important than that, it would bring you into contact with the staff, *on an informal basis.* However *devoted* a mother is . . . and I'm sure your mother *is* devoted . . .'

Colin blinked.

'She can never do for a boy what a man can do. It needs a man to . . .' Mr Sawdon took a deep breath, perhaps remembering Colin's age, 'to ensure that a boy's development is . . . healthy. *Normal.*'

*

Why do you dress as a woman?

BERNARD

A joke. A couple of blokes at work bet me I couldn't get away with it . . . (*Shrugs*) That's all there was to it.

VON STROHM

Names?

Silence.

The names of the 'blokes' at work?

Silence.

There's no reason to protect them. A joke is not a crime. We Germans are famous for our sense of humour.

He waits, but it's obvious Bernard is not going to speak.

Stand up.

Bernard's face tightens. The talking is over.

Hold the chair above your head.

Bernard hesitates, then obeys. Von Strohm leans against the table, watching. There is a clock on the wall behind him. As Bernard, his face set, continues to hold the chair above his head, the clock face blurs. When it clears, two hours have passed.

VON STROHM
(*Conversationally, as if asking the question for the first time*)
Why do you dress as a woman?

BERNARD

A . . . joke.

He sways, and seems about to fall. Von Strohm walks across to him, leans in close.

Are you listening?

By some trick of the light, Bernard is reflected in von Strohm's glasses. A double image, tiny and powerless.

'I said, Are you listening?'
  'Yes, Sir.'
  'Well, you certainly didn't look as if you were.' Mr Sawdon leant back in his chair. 'We've agreed then that you're going to get to bed every night at a reasonable hour?'
  'Yes, Sir.'
  'And that you're going to make a real effort to join in more with the life of the school.'
  'Yes, Sir.'
  'Good. And I'll see you again at the end of next week and we'll see how things are going.'
  'Yes. Thank you, Sir.'
  Colin had got to the door, before Mr Sawdon spoke again. 'Oh and Harper, I think perhaps I ought to have a word with your mother. There'll be a letter in the post on Monday.'

Bernard, face glistening with sweat, still holds the chair above his head, but now a subtle change is taking place.

VON STROHM

Why do you . . .

BERNARD

All right! All right!

He tries to lower the chair, but a gesture from von Strohm stops him.

It . . . it comes over me. I try not to. I sit there night after night . . . I've even thrown away the key to the wardrobe, and then it comes over me again, and I go and break the lock. I used to just do it at home, you know, and that was all right. A bit lonely, but at least I didn't get into trouble, but then I got this urge to go and walk the streets . . .

Cries.

I've been like it all my life. Ever since I was twelve years old . . . You see, I never had a father. There was no *male* influence. Nothing *healthy*. Nothing *normal*. I never even joined the boy scouts. And I used to . . .

He struggles to hold back the final degradation, but it's no use.

I used to wear my sister's knickers.

Bernard is now a snivelling wreck, cheeks streaked with mascara, courage, pride, manhood gone.
    A long silence.
    Then von Strohm, leaning against the table, begins to clap. Not a spontaneous burst of applause, but a slow, hard, ironical clapping . . .

that follows Colin down the corridor, as he half-runs, half-walks to his next lesson.

9

The cloakroom was crowded with boys, jostling in the cramped space as they pulled on shorts, or jumped about on one foot, fumbling with knotted laces. Mr Bellingham, a bull-necked, white-haired man in his fifties, stood in the doorway, speaking sharply to any boy who appeared to be loitering.

The double swing doors burst open, and Colin skidded to a halt.

'Late again, Harper?'

'I had to see Mr Sawdon, Sir.'

'What about?'

'Being late, Sir.'

Mr Bellingham closed his eyes. 'Why did I ask that?' He opened them again. 'Well, go on then, get ready. Don't just stand there.' Raising his voice, he turned to the rest of the class. 'Lesson'll be over before some of you lot get started.'

Colin began to get undressed.

Mr Bellingham looked round the room. Lorrimer still had his shirt on.

'Why aren't you changed, Lorrimer?'

'I am changed, Sir.'

Lorrimer was very fat with a rather high-pitched voice. At the sound of it, some of the other boys exchanged bright, alert, salivating glances.

'Don't argue with me, lad. You are not *changed*. *Changed*, you are not.'

Lorrimer's watery grey eyes slid away.

'Where's your football shirt?'

'Haven't got one, Sir.'

'Gym shirt?'

'Haven't brought it, Sir.'

'Why not?'

"Tisn't gym, Sir.'

'Are you trying to be funny?'

'No, Sir.'

Mr Bellingham took a deep breath. '*Why* haven't you got a football shirt?'

'Forgot it, Sir.'

'Lorrimer, you're hopeless. What are you?'

'Hopeless.'

'Hopeless, what?'

'Hopeless, *Sir*.'

Colin had gone to the same junior school as Lorrimer. They'd been the only two to pass the eleven plus, and, on the first day of term, Lorrimer had called for Colin and they'd walked to Queen Elizabeth's together, both frightened, both pretending not to be.

'It's every lesson the same, isn't it? "Forgot it, Sir." "Can't find it, Sir." "Three bags full, Sir."'

The boys tittered at the lisping, effeminate imitation, though it didn't sound anything like Lorrimer. Lorrimer didn't lisp – he squeaked.

'Well, I'm full too, Lorrimer, full up to here.' Mr Bellingham tapped his forehead with the side of his hand. 'I don't think there's been *one* week since you started this school – not one week – that you've had your full kit. *Detention*. And get that shirt off. You can play in your vest.'

'I'll catch me death, Sir.'

'Lorrimer, this is September, not January. You will not "catch your death".' He looked round the room. 'And the rest of you get a move on. I want everybody out of this building before I finish counting ten.' Making chopping movements with his hand, he began to count. 'One. Two. Three.' A boy, his arm raised, came running, but Mr Bellingham merely lowered his head and bellowed: 'FOUR!'

By 'seven', most of the boys were outside, lined up for the short walk to the football field. By 'ten', only Lorrimer remained inside. Mr Bellingham, his back propping the door open, started a slow handclap.

At last Lorrimer emerged, slowly, an inch at a time, chafing his crossed arms and squinting at the sky.

'Get a move on!'

Lorrimer lowered his arms, to reveal plump breasts bulging through the holes in his string vest. Several of the boys wolf-whistled.

'All right,' Mr Bellingham said. 'That'll do.'

But he was grinning as he said it. None of the boys took any notice, but continued to clap, as Lorrimer, red-faced and on the verge of tears, walked to the back of the line.

*

In the Gestapo interrogation room, von Strohm's slow handclap continues. Bernard, his face a mess of sweat and melted make-up, gazes wildly around him.

The walls are lined with boys in football shirts and shorts. They stare at Bernard, joining in the slow handclap, the smack of flesh on flesh becoming louder, and louder again, carrying with it the unmistakable threat of violence.

'Hurry up!'

Backing onto the football pitch, Mr Bellingham blew his whistle, waving to the stragglers. Half-heartedly, they started to run. Lorrimer brought up the rear, already out of breath, one hand pressed to a stitch in his side.

'C'mon now, line up. Abbott and Kennedy, you pick the teams. Abbott, you start. And don't take all day about it. It's not the World Cup.' He turned away, muttering, 'God help England if it was.'

Kennedy's hand shot up. 'It's not fair, Sir. Abbott always picks first.'

Mr Bellingham bared his teeth in a grin. 'Well, his name always begins with "A", doesn't it?'

Abbott got in quickly. 'Harper.'

'Watson.'

The names were called out, each name reducing the number of unselected boys until only Lorrimer was left.

'You see?' Kennedy complained, to nobody in particular. 'It's every week the same. Every bleeding week.'

Abbott and his team were already jogging away up the field.

VON STROHM

You know, Bernard, you and I would get on *so* much better if you would only stop insulting my intelligence. You don't dress as a woman because of some . . . *disgusting* personal problem.

You do it because women carry fewer identity papers – therefore a lower chance of being found out. *And* they're not liable to forced labour. *They* don't have to work in the docks.

BERNARD

Surely if I was a spy I would *want* to work in the docks?

VON STROHM
(*waves the objection aside*)

Oh, there are a lot of advantages to being a woman, if you can get away with it. It makes life so much easier, don't you think?

He leans forward.

I want the names of all the British agents working in this area. And don't tell me there aren't any, because I know there are.

Think, Bernard. You owe no loyalty to British agents. What have they ever done, except get Frenchmen killed? If you give me the names of the British agents, it may be possible to spare your own people. Otherwise . . .

Bernard remains silent.

Von Strohm sighs, elaborately, and gestures to somebody behind him. Men in uniform line the walls, among them the bull-necked figure of Mr Bellingham.

Von Strohm turns fastidiously away, as they crowd in round Bernard and kick him to the floor. Bernard rolls on his side to get away from their boots, but there is no escape.

Thuds, and grunts of effort . . .

A knot of struggling feet. Colin couldn't see what was happening, but then Kennedy got the ball, and Colin fell back to cover his goal. *C'mon*, he thought. Jenkins was left standing. Abbott got close, but then Kennedy whipped the ball out to the left. Past lumbering Dodds – casually, almost cruelly, past him — and that left Colin. He came out fast, narrowing the angle, holding himself back. *Wait*, he told himself. He saw Kennedy's eyes tense, and started to spread himself.

At full stretch, he thought it was going in, but he got his fingers to it — just — and deflected it past the net. He got up, wiping his muddy hands on the front of his shorts, and did his best to look as if the outcome had never been in doubt.

Bernard lies on the cellar floor.

VON STROHM
(*sympathetically*)

Face facts, Bernard. We know your identity papers are forged, we know you're with the Resistance.

Bernard moans, trying to open his swollen eyes.

You've got nothing to reproach yourself with. You've held out long enough. Only there's no point going on.

He sits on the edge of the table, looking down at Bernard.

I don't like these methods any more than you do. But I'll use them, if that's the only way I can get what I want.

He gets up to go, but at the door turns and looks back.

Names, Bernard. *Names.*

In the other goal, like a reflection in a fairground mirror, Lorrimer chafed his arms to keep warm. Putting him in goal, when he so obviously didn't care whether the ball went in or not, was stupid, Colin thought. Kennedy only did it because Lorrimer was big, and he couldn't think where else to put him. But it was losing them the match.

Resigned to not seeing the ball again, Colin patrolled the

edge of his penalty area. He liked goalkeeping. He liked the feeling of being in sole charge of his own small patch, part of the team, but not submerged in it. Or rather, when things were going well, he liked it. On the days when Kennedy seemed incapable of putting a foot wrong, and sent ball after ball flying past him, he didn't like it at all. But so far this term there hadn't been a day like that.

Mr Bellingham was staring at him. He tried to look busy, pressing down an imaginary ruck. But it wasn't easy to look busy, when the ball was nowhere in sight. It was a relief when the whistle blew.

Mr Bellingham was waiting for him in the corridor outside the changing room. 'Good save,' he said.

Colin mumbled something about luck.

'No, you took your time, you narrowed him down . . . I've had my eye on you for a while.' He tapped Colin on the shoulder. 'Tomorrow, two o'clock.'

He was already walking away along the corridor.

'What for, Sir?'

'The under-fourteens, of course.'

He hadn't even bothered to turn round.

Colin swallowed hard. 'I can't, Sir.'

'What do you mean, you can't?'

'I play football with me mates on Saturday, Sir.'

'Your mates?' Mr Bellingham came all the way back and towered over him. 'Harper, do you realize how many boys in this school would give their *eye teeth* to be in the under-fourteens?'

'Yes, Sir.'

'Well, then?'

'Yes, Sir.'

Colin was tempted to skip showers. He sat on the bench, and unlaced his football boots, slowly. The changing room smelled of wet towels, wet hair, wet skin. A smell he normally liked, but today it made him feel sick.

Mr Bellingham scanned the room. 'Anybody not had a shower? Harper?'

'Just going, Sir.'

'Lorrimer?'

Lorrimer was fully dressed.

'Sir?'

'Showers, Lorrimer. Have you had a shower?'

'Yes, Sir.'

Mr Bellingham smiled. 'Anybody here see Lorrimer in the showers?'

Gradually conversations stopped and the boys turned to face him.

'Abbott? You see him?'

'No, Sir.'

'Kennedy?'

'No, Sir.'

Lorrimer glared at them. 'I did have one, Sir.'

Mr Bellingham tapped him on the head. 'Carrying an umbrella, were we?' He waited for his laugh, and got it. 'Clothes off, lad, and quick about it. And for heaven's *sake*, Lorrimer, if you're going to tell lies, tell them with a bit more intelligence than that.'

Lorrimer sat on the bench beside Colin, and started to unlace his shoes. 'It isn't fair.'

'Why isn't it?' Colin reached for his towel. 'Everybody else has to have one.'

'I've got a bad chest,' Lorrimer called out after him.

It had nothing to do with his chest, unless 'chest' meant tits. Everybody knew why Lorrimer tried to dodge showers.

Cold water fracturing itself on the nape of his neck, Colin shut out awareness of what was happening further along. Kennedy and one or two other members of the losing team, had pinned Lorrimer's arms behind him and were holding his face under the jet. Blue-faced and gasping, he was allowed up for air, only to be pushed back under.

Bernard, hair and clothes drenched, lies in a heap of straw, his teeth chattering with cold. Footsteps. Painfully, he turns to face the door. Two guards enter, kicking a small, dark man down the steps.

ANTOINE

Pigs!

One of the guards, stung by the insult, comes the rest of the way down the steps, and deliberately grinds his boot into Antoine's hand. The door clangs shut. Cradling his hand, Antoine crawls towards Bernard.

ANTOINE
(*holds out his good hand*)

Antoine.

Bernard nods, but ignores the hand. He has watched the whole incident with more suspicion than sympathy.

ANTOINE

That's right, be cautious. You're right. You can't be too careful in here.

BERNARD

I've got nothing to be cautious about. They arrested me by mistake.

ANTOINE

That's right, you stick to your story, but I know who you are. The guards are full of it. Bernard. The famous Bernard. Hero of the Resistance.

BERNARD

So *that's* who they think I am!

An inspiration to us all.

Bernard's bland expression doesn't change. Antoine appears to come to a decision. He starts pulling off his shirt.

ANTOINE

Look.

His back is horribly scarred by repeated floggings. Bernard's expression changes. He offers his hand.

BERNARD

I'm sorry I doubted you.

ANTOINE

No, you were right to be cautious. There are traitors everywhere.

Everywhere. Everywhere. Antoine's voice bounced off the white-tiled walls. *People you would never suspect . . .*

Colin's arm ached, with cold, he thought, but then he looked down, and saw five raised, red marks, each one surmounted by blisters that, when he pressed them, oozed a clear, yellowish fluid. No hand could have done that. Even if you held somebody really hard, he thought, hard enough to make them cry out, it still wouldn't do that.

Further along, Lorrimer broke free, and yelled, 'I could've *drowned.*'

Kennedy leant against the tiles, laughing.

Lorrimer, pink and raw-looking, mouth slobbery with cold, started to push past Colin. 'I'll fetch me dad.'

'Go on, then.'

'Aw shurrup, Lorrimer,' Colin said. 'You're always fetching your dad.'

Lorrimer turned to him. 'At least I've got one to fetch.'

A startled silence. Colin looked at Kennedy, but Kennedy was already turning away.

Rats infest the cellar where Bernard and Antoine lie huddled in the straw, rats whose sleek fur and bright eyes seem to mock the condition of the men.

Antoine looks much as he did before, but Bernard has been beaten up again. Only now, instead of enduring his pain in lonely silence, he's talking eagerly to Antoine.

ANTOINE

Are you sure you didn't give anything away?

BERNARD

Positive. Von Strohm knows he got nothing out of that.

ANTOINE

That's the third time, though. They won't give up.

BERNARD

How did you get on?

ANTOINE
(*evasively*)

All right, I suppose.

BERNARD

He seemed to know more than he did last time . . .
The questions had more point to them.

ANTOINE

Perhaps they've captured another agent.

Bernard sits brooding for a moment. He glances across at Antoine.

BERNARD

That isn't the only possibility.

Antoine looks frightened. He licks his lips, and glances towards the door.

BERNARD

So it *was* you.

He throws himself on Antoine and starts to throttle him. Antoine manages to free himself, momentarily.

ANTOINE

They've got my son.

Bernard does not immediately let go, but then, gradually, doubt and hesitation enter his face. He lowers his hands.

BERNARD

You do realize, don't you, that if I tell them I know you're a traitor, they'll kill you *and* your son?

ANTOINE
(*holding his throat*)

Yes, I know.

Bernard stares at him, pity struggling with contempt.

BERNARD

Relax, Antoine. I'm not going to tell them. You can go on doing exactly what you have been doing. Reporting back every word I say.

ANTOINE

What are you going to do?

BERNARD

You mean, what am I going to say?

A malicious glint.

I'm going to give them names – or rather, *you*'re going to give them names – of one or two collaborators, people we've been wanting rid of for some time.

He looks sombrely at Antoine – and now pity is uppermost.

You see, Antoine, we're all going to die – you and me *and* your son – there's no way out for any of us – but we may as well take one or two of the rats with us when we go.

10

Colin's nan was sitting in the armchair by the fire when he got in from school.

'Hello, son,' she said, and then, predictably, to Viv, 'By, he hasn't half grown. He'll be in men's sizes, isn't he?'

'Don't I know it. Your dinner's on top of the grill, Colin.'

'Of course your father had big feet.'

Colin got his dinner — sausage and chips — and sat at the table to eat it. At the other end of the room, the conversation continued, if you could call it a conversation when one person did all the talking.

'I said to her, "Lilian," I said. "You're a fool." She says, "How am I? I've got four spare bedrooms up there – they still have to be done out and dusted whether there's anybody in them or not. I might just as well have the money. Particularly," she says, "with the Hippodrome just down the road." That was it, you see, she was fancying herself as a theatrical landlady. She always had a hankering for the bright lights. "Suit yourself," I said, "Personally, I wouldn't fancy somebody else's knickers dripping into *my* frying pan." "Oh," she says, "they're not all like that." "No," I says, "some of them are men." But of course that wouldn't put *her* off. Anybody else with a teenage daughter in the house'd stop and think, but not our Lilian.'

Rather desperately, Colin thought, Viv broke in. 'Do they know who the father is?'

How could she sit there and ask that?

'The pantomime horse, would you believe? Aladdin. The back end. Of course it's the baby you have to feel sorry for. Poor little mite.'

Colin found it difficult to feel sorry for any baby whose father could be as precisely located as that.

'How far on is she?' Viv asked.

'Lilian's got her reckoned up to eight month. "Aladdin closed in February," she says. Well, I took one look at the girl and I thought, Aye, and it opened in December. But I didn't say anything. I mean, for all I know she's carrying a lot of water. And all you can get out of Enid is, "Will it be normal?" Well, you see, she's swallowed such a load of stuff. I says, "Look, honey, if you'd seen the amount of stuff our Viv swallowed you'd've done no more good. And she didn't stop at taking stuff either, she went to that woman in Crathorne Road, and yet the baby was all right." She says, "Well, I don't know. I don't think it can do any good." I says, "Enid. If it did any harm there'd be half the bloody country walking round with bits missing." '

Colin wondered what the stuff was that Viv had swallowed,

and what the woman in Crathorne Road had done, and whether this had anything to do with the shape of his ears.

'I suppose there's no prospect of him marrying her?' Viv said.

'Married already.'

'Poor lass.'

'I told Lilian, I says, "That's what you get for having daughters." I says to her, "You want to pray for a lad." She says, "It doesn't matter what it is, she's having it adopted." I says, "Aye, that's easy said. Now, when you haven't even seen it. I can't see you, our Lilian, giving away your own flesh and blood." '

'But it's not up to her, is it? She's not having it.'

'No, but it'll be her that carries the can.'

'And it'll be Enid that has to live it down. And if you want *my* opinion the best thing she can do is have it adopted. And then move right away, where nobody knows her. Because if she stays here, there'll always be some kind soul to throw it up at her.'

'And could *you* live with that? Not knowing where the bairn was, and whether it had a bite to eat in its mouth?'

'For God's sake, Mam. What kind of homes do you think they put them in? It wouldn't just have a bite to eat. It'd have a nice home, a mother *and* a father to bring it up. Probably a brother or a sister. A start in life.'

Silence. His nan's eyes were like black coals.

'Shall I put the kettle on?' Colin said.

'Aye, go on, son,' Viv said, visibly trying to calm herself down. 'You'll have one, Mam, won't you?'

Colin went into the kitchen and switched the kettle on. In the next room, the voices started again. He waited till the steam was rising from the spout, and then put his hand in close, to feel the pain.

*

*Rats run across the floor of the cellar where Bernard is imprisoned,
even scuttling across his feet. But now it can be seen that the rats are
entering and leaving the cellar by a grille, set into the wall at floor
level.*

*On the heap of straw, Bernard lies awake. From his appearance,
he seems to have been beaten up again. He also, perhaps, has a
slight fever. As he stares around the room, objects begin to blur and
shift.*

A scuffling sound, coming nearer.

*Bernard, lifting his head, looks towards the grille. On the other
side, in the semi-darkness, an eye gleams. The scratching sound is
repeated. Then, just as Bernard is about to lower his head, a human
hand appears and gropes through the bars.*

GASTON

Bernard.

Grunting with pain, Bernard crawls across to the grille.

Can you help me move this?

*They struggle with the grille, but it is too firmly embedded in the
stone to be shifted by a boy and a badly weakened man.*

I'll have to come back. I'll bring Pierre.

BERNARD

I'm not alone, you know. There's Antoine.

GASTON

Is he reliable?

BERNARD
(*laughs*)

Anything but. He's with them at the moment. I've been trying
to feed them false information through him, but that won't
last for ever.

Gaston passes a knife through the bars.

Wait till you hear us coming.

Bernard takes the knife, glances towards Antoine's sleeping place, and then slowly nods.

'I know what they say about me behind my back, don't think I don't,' Viv said. '*Waitress*? Not what they called it in our young day. They want to be in here some nights when I come in from work, and have a look at me feet. You don't get feet like that lying on your back.'

'You still seeing him?' Nan asked.

'Who?'

'You know who.'

'I can hardly avoid seeing him, Mam. He's the manager.'

Nan waited.

'We do have the occasional night out. Yes.'

'And he's still living with his wife?'

'Yes. But he says he can't stand it much longer. She hasn't half played Hamlet with him.'

'Oh and what's he been playing? Apart from away from home.'

'A man can't do right with you, can he, Mam?'

'I just wish you'd face facts. A man like that isn't going to leave his wife. Apart from anything else, when the old man goes she stands to inherit the business. Do you think he's going to walk out on that? And take on the upkeep of somebody else's kid?'

Viv looked away. 'Colin, isn't it time you were going back to school?'

Colin had decided on the way home that he couldn't face going back to school. 'I don't feel very well, Mam. Me arm aches.'

'There's many a night my heart aches, but I still have to go to work.'

'What's the matter with his arm? What's the matter, son?'

'I don't know. I've just got these funny spots.'

'Let's have a look.' She rolled his sleeve up. 'Aw, howay, Viv, you can't send him to school with that.'

'Why, what d'you think it is?'

'Well, it looks like erysipelas, doesn't it? But I don't suppose it is. Anyway, it starts on your scalp. How do you feel, son?'

Colin was about to say 'all right', but stopped himself in time. 'Not too good.'

'You want to get him down the doctor's, our Viv.'

'You can't just walk in, Mam. You have to make an appointment.'

'So go and make one. I'll stop with him.'

Viv looked doubtful. 'All right,' she said at last.

After she'd gone, Colin said, 'What's ery . . . ?'

'Erysipelas. Your mam had it when she was a bairn. She used to call it Harry syphilis.' She laughed. 'Mind, she did have it bad. You know, there wasn't the antibiotics and stuff in them days, and oh dear me . . . Her mind started wandering. I was at me wit's end, and all I could get out of her was, "*I want me dad. I want me dad.*" And, of course, that was the winter he buggered off and left us. Anyway, I thought, I can't have this, so I put me hat and coat on, and I went round, like to where I knew he was living. Oh, and *she* answered the door. You know, she wasn't smart, she hadn't a bit of style about her . . . Nothing. But still. He found something in her he didn't find in me. But the Harpers were all a bit like that, you know. Very *sensual*.

'Anyway. I was that flummoxed seeing her stood there, I give *her* the message. And I didn't mince words, either. I thought we'd got beyond that. I says, "Tell him his daughter's dying, and if he wants to see her again, he'd better get himself round quick." Well, whether she passed it on or not, I don't know, but anyway he never come. I waited and waited, and at the finish I locked the door and went to bed.

'Anyway, the next morning the fever had broke. And I didn't know what to say for the best. I says, "I'm sorry your dad didn't come, flower. I did go round." And she just looks at me, and she says, "What do you mean? He was here all night." I says, "No, flower, you've dreamt it," but she says, "Mam. He was here." She says, "He never left me."'

'How old was she?'

'Nine. Eight when he left. Oh and she idolized her dad. Mind, and he did her. That's why I think the old cow never give him the message. He'd've come if he'd known. But, anyway, he died not long after, so we never found out the rights and wrongs of it.'

'She never mentions him.'

'No, she wouldn't. We went to the funeral, and I was stood on one side of the grave, with my kids, and *she* was stood on the other, with her kids. Five of them, and all grown up. You couldn't accuse him of chasing spring chicken, my God, you couldn't. Anyway we come home, and your mam was very quiet. No funeral tea, of course. That was all round *her* house, and then all of a sudden your mam says, "Can I have tuppence for the pictures?" I says, "You can't go to the pictures tonight, honey." But she got it out of me. And she *went* to the pictures. And do you know, that was the first time I thought, *Viv, I don't know what makes you tick*, but my God, it wasn't the last.' She stared into the grate. 'You know, you'd've liked your grandad, Colin. I wish you could've met him.'

'I wish I could've met me dad.'

'Ah, well.'

'Didn't she ever say anything?'

'*No*. And it wasn't for want of asking, I can tell you. I says, "Why should he get off scot-free? It's just as much his bairn as it is yours." But no. "*No*," she says, "I'll manage." Aye, I thought, muggins'll manage. And believe you me, muggins did.'

Footsteps outside in the passage.

'Nine o'clock, Tuesday,' Viv said, coming into the room. 'That's the earliest I could get.' She stopped, and looked at them. 'Been having a little chat?'

'Yes, Colin's been telling me all about his school, haven't you, Colin? I always said you were a bright lad. Didn't I, Viv? You know when you were a baby, Colin, we took you to the doctor, and your mam says, "Look at his head." And he says, "Why, what's the matter with his head?" She says, "Well, it's a funny shape." And he says, "Oh, don't you worry about that." He says, "My lad's got a head shaped like that and he's at the university." '

'I think it'd be a good idea to get some elastoplast on that arm, Colin,' Viv said. 'Stop it oozing on your shirt. I think there's some upstairs in the bathroom cabinet.'

Colin went slowly upstairs, trying to imagine what it would be like to have been adopted. But, of course, you couldn't imagine it. Instead of Nan and Viv and Pauline and Mrs Hennigan, there was just a circle of blank faces.

As he turned from the bathroom cabinet, he caught sight of himself in the mirror. A flaw ran the whole length of the glass, and, for a moment, he played with it, bobbing from side to side, making his forehead first bulge and then recede.

Even when he stopped doing that, his face didn't look normal. It'd changed quite a lot in the last few months, and that wasn't just his imagination, because other people had noticed, too. All the bones jutted out more. It felt almost as if another face was pushing its way to the surface, somebody else's face, and he didn't know whose.

He went into his bedroom, and lay on the bed, and listened, as he'd listened many times before, to the sound of women's voices, bringing memories out of their shared store. And, as always, this work of remembering, so careful, so detailed, so intricate, left one enormous gap.

He put his hands to his ears, and shut the voices out.

11

The house seemed very quiet after his nan had gone home. Colin went downstairs and sat on the sofa by the fire. Viv was ironing. He closed his eyes, listening to the thump-thump of the iron on the board, and the sizzle of spit, as Viv tapped the base. 'I'm going to get meself an electric iron out of Pauline's catalogue,' she said. 'This bloody thing belongs in a museum.'

'You going out tonight?'

'I'm going to work.'

'No, I meant after.' He meant, Are you bringing Reg home? Though it hardly mattered what he meant since Viv didn't bother to answer. 'I've got nothing to *do*.'

'Should've gone to school.'

'I'm not well enough for school.'

'Aw, pull the other one, Colin.'

'I'm not. Nan said she thought it might be erysipelas.'

'Like hell.'

He'd only said it because he hoped it might make her talk about her father. Even if *his* father was unmentionable, he didn't see why *hers* should be. But she never had talked about him, and he knew she never would. It was a bit like Russian dolls. You unscrewed first one and then another, and so on into the centre, and each doll was smaller than the one before, and the last face of all was blank.

'Mam,' he said. 'Did you ever think of having me adopted?'

Viv's face went smooth. 'What makes you ask that?'

'I just wondered. Nan said Enid wants hers adopted.'

'She's plenty of time to change her mind.' Viv hung one shirt over the back of the chair, and started to iron the next. 'There's no point me pretending you were wanted, Colin, because you weren't. But we did love you once you were here.'

'We', he noted. Not 'I'. He would have given anything for her to have said 'I'.

'You'll understand when you're older.'

He understood already, more than he was ever given credit for, and more than he wanted to understand. Viv had wanted him adopted; his nan had insisted on keeping him. But Viv had been right, he thought, or at least she had been right *for her*. She could have been married by now, with other children, and a home of her own.

The thought sharpened him against her. 'Nan thinks you're a fool for bothering with Reg, doesn't she?'

'Colin. *Uncle* Reg or *Mister* Boyce. You're not old enough to call him anything else.'

Try me.

Colin looked around the room, at the worn patches on the

lino, at the fireplace with its two cracked tiles, and at the walls, whose pattern of roses on a trellis had long since faded to a dingy beige. Everything seemed to have shrunk around him, to pull across his shoulders, like a jumper he'd grown out of. He wanted to sweep it all away.

Bernard sits with his back to the wall, fighting to stay awake. He looks towards the grille, but there's still no sign of rescue. The room begins to blur, and Bernard jerks himself upright.

Viv sighed. 'You know, Colin, if you've got nothing better to do, you might just as well nip down the shops for me.'

'I can't. Somebody'd see me.'

'They wouldn't. They're not out of school yet. And anyway, nobody round here goes to your school.'

'All right. What do you want?'

'Quarter of boiled ham, half a dozen eggs and tell her I'll pay her tomorrow.'

On the front doorstep, Colin paused, looking up and down the road. A smell of flowering privet, baking in the heat. A smell that, for some reason, always excited him. He was *free*. There was no need to hurry back. Viv was only too pleased to have him out of the way.

Bernard jerks himself awake again, looking towards the grille. A scuffling sound. And then two pale faces appear behind the bars. Gaston and Pierre.

Gaston nods towards Antoine who's asleep in the straw. Bernard takes out the knife and, with an expression almost of regret, bends over him. There is no sound.

PIERRE

All right?

As right as murder ever is.

PIERRE

Bring some of the straw. If the grille falls on your side, there'll be a hell of a row.

GASTON

Enough to wake the dead.

And, unexpectedly, he giggles.

'What's amusing you?'

Colin jumped. 'A quarter of boiled ham, please.' He waited till she'd wrapped it. 'And could you put it on the book, please?'

Mrs Blue Rinse looked at him. Slowly, she reached for the ledger, flicked the pages till she got to 'H' and then, licking her stub of pencil, said, 'Tell her, there's two pound, eleven and six owing. And accounts are supposed to be settled on *Friday*.'

He had been going to buy himself some sweets, but it didn't seem to be the right moment.

'I'll tell her,' he said.

Pierre, Gaston and Bernard emerge from the tunnel into the moonlit forest. They look around them, and then pause in the shadow of the trees to take stock of their situation.

GASTON

How long before they know you're gone?

BERNARD

It's impossible to say. They keep the interrogation times deliberately random. Sometimes it's two or three times a night. At other times . . .

GASTON

So we don't know how long we've got.

PIERRE

More to the point, do we know where we're going?

GASTON

The café.

PIERRE

Are you crazy? German soldiers in the bar. The Kommandant in Vivienne's bedroom.

GASTON

That's one place they won't look.

PIERRE

Well, it's my café, and I say no.

BERNARD

I'm quite happy to move on. You know the last thing I want is to put anybody else at risk. All I need is a change of clothes. I've already got a spare set of identity papers.

GASTON

Where?

BERNARD

It's better you don't know.

GASTON

All right. Pierre, he'll have to change clothes in the café, but that'll only take a couple of hours. We'll move him to a safe house as soon as it's dark. If there are any safe houses left.

BERNARD

What do you mean?

GASTON

We don't know how much information that little rat passed on before you realized he was a traitor.

He wasn't a rat, he was a man who loved his son. And he passed nothing on because I told him nothing. You see, in my eyes, Gaston, everybody is a potential traitor. Everybody has a breaking point. Everybody has a price.

An uncomfortable silence.

GASTON

Do you include yourself in this, Bernard?

BERNARD

But of course.

A coil and hiss of dead leaves. Colin looked back along the avenue of trees, and saw how individual leaves, fluttering down, stained the air gold.

A great pile of them had collected in a corner by one of the benches, and he started to kick them about, releasing the dark odour of decay. An enormous black beetle ran out of the heap, and Colin dropped to his knees to watch it go.

He looked up, and along the avenue of trees again. He couldn't shake off a feeling of sadness. The dead leaves, the smell of decay, even this golden light that could never be mistaken for the light of spring or summer . . .

He began walking down the steps towards the open-air theatre. He'd seen picture postcards of the theatre in its heyday, with bands playing, and ladies in long skirts and feathered hats, but that had been a long time ago. Nobody ever came here now. It was very quiet, and dark, a bowl brimming with darkness, and when you stood on the stage and looked up the rows of empty chairs to the trees and the grass and the golden light, they seemed to belong to another world.

He heard the footsteps before he saw the person making

them. All sounds were magnified here, by the shape of the theatre, but every sound produced a multitude of echoes, and so, for a long time, Colin couldn't be sure where the noise was coming from.

And then he saw him, on the lip of the bowl, a black, tall figure, just passing from light to darkness. He came down the steps at the side of the theatre, the same way that Colin had come, feeling his way slowly from step to step, his eyes not yet adjusted to the darkness.

Colin glanced rapidly from side to side, wishing he'd stayed at the other end of the park, near the tennis courts and the boating lake, where even on a Friday afternoon there would have been other people around. At the same time he knew he wasn't in that kind of danger, and that other people would be no help at all.

He was closer now, beginning to climb the steps at the side of the stage. Colin hid in the shadows, waiting for him to appear.

First the head came bobbing up the steps, and then the shoulders, and then the rest of him, until he was standing on the stage, looking out over the rows of empty seats – and giving no sign that he was aware of the twelve-year-old boy behind him.

Colin was afraid that the intensity of his stare would attract the man's attention. He forced himself to turn away, to look at the wall instead. Level with his eyes was a web, with flies in neat bundles, and a slim spider waiting.

He looked again at the man, who stood on the very edge of the stage, his toes pointing over the drop. Something in the blackness of that shape drew Colin towards it. He began to walk forward, quietly, but making no real effort not to be heard, until he was close enough to see the whiteness of the collar, the slight reddening of the skin above it, the way the dark blond hair curled into the nape of the neck.

Slowly, as if for the first time the man was aware of being

observed, the head began to turn. But before he could see the face, Colin had cried out, and was running down the steps, and back along the avenue of trees.

He heard footsteps following him, but perhaps it was only the echo of his own, because when he turned and looked back he could see nobody, only shafts of golden light slanting down, and the black bars of the trees.

He sat down on the grass and pressed his hands together between his knees, and rocked, amazed to find himself shaking.

12

'*D*id you and me mam know each other during the war?' Colin asked.

'Why, aye,' said Pauline. 'We joined up together. And what a job we had, didn't we? At least I had. Do you know, I cut the coupon out of the paper twice, and each time me mam tore it up? She says, "You're not joining the ATS. I don't mind you working in a factory, but you're not joining that." '

'My mam was the same,' Viv said. 'But a lot of people were like that about the ATS, weren't they? And right through the war, too. It started to get a little bit better after Princess Elizabeth joined up.'

'Yeah, that's right. They couldn't very well accuse *her* of going behind the NAAFI. It used to get on my wick, though, didn't it you? You know, Colin, we were on the guns at the chemical works. And some nights you didn't even get your uniform on. You were stuck out there in these bloody awful pyjamas and a steel hat rammed down on top of your curlers, and ooh it didn't half hurt. And yet to hear people talk you were having some kind of . . . of . . .'

'Orgy,' said Viv.

'That's it.'

'Did you fire the guns?' Colin asked.

'No, the women weren't supposed to do that. In fact where we were, the men weren't supposed to hit anything. You were meant to shoot under them, and push them up off the target. Eeh, but one night – do you remember, Viv? – we got one. Oh, and we were over the moon.'

'You should've seen her,' said Viv. 'She was doing a war dance.'

'Well, we all were. And then the sergeant – eeh, dear me, I'll never forget it.' She put her hand over her mouth to hide a grin. 'He came down on us like a ton of bricks. He says, "What the bloody hell do you think you're doing? Do you realize what would happen if a bomber landed on them works? The whole bloody town'd go up." Oh, and we just looked at each other, 'cause of course we knew he was right. "Next time you do that," he says, "you're back in that kitchen, and as far as I'm concerned you can wash dishes for the rest of the war." But, anyway, we were lucky, he come down in a field. And even that . . . The whole sky was lit up.' Her face was lit up, too. 'Eeh, it's a terrible thing to say, isn't it, but I wouldn't've missed it for the world.'

'No, nor me. In fact, I think the first two years of the war were the happiest years of my life.'

*

Bernard is sitting in front of the dressing table, looking at his reflection in the triple mirror. Paulette is searching through the wardrobe.

BERNARD

I thought I'd said goodbye to all this.

PAULETTE

I just hope I can find something that'll fit you. Here, look, what about this?

She holds up a red dress.

BERNARD

It's a bit bright, isn't it? I don't want to attract attention.

PAULETTE

Yeah, but it's got an elasticated waist. You're going to need all the give you can get. Where do you usually get your dresses?

BERNARD

My sister. She's a big woman.

PAULETTE

She must be. Mind you, Vivienne's a size sixteen. You wouldn't think it to look at her, but she is.

She turns her back while Bernard struggles into the red dress, and adjusts the blonde wig.

Well, it's not perfect, but I don't think we'll do any better. Anyway, it's time we were off.

BERNARD

It's good of you to take the risk.

PAULETTE

You'll be safer with me than you would be on your own. Right then, are you ready?

*

'If I can find me shoes, I am.'

'Under the table,' Colin said.

Viv knelt and groped. 'What do you think of these?' she said, holding up a pair of black, patent-leather sling-backs. 'I got them in the sale at Barratts.'

'Very nice. I'm surprised you can walk in them, mind.'

'We're not going to walk. We . . . we're getting a lift.'

'Reg? Ooh, I am honoured.'

A car horn sounded in the street.

'That'll be him now. You'll be all right, won't you, Colin? Mrs Hennigan's in.'

'No, she isn't,' Colin said.

'Oh, my God, *Friday*.' She looked at Pauline. 'Spuggy night. Well, Colin, there's nothing I can do. If you don't want to stop in on your own, you'll just have to go with her. Or ask Ross if he wants to come around.'

'I'll be all right.'

At the door Viv paused, and looked back, as if she'd suddenly lost her nerve. 'Do I look all right?' she said.

'You look smashing,' Pauline said, firmly, pushing Viv ahead of her through the door.

An upstairs room in the café. Gaston lifts the lace curtain, and watches as Bernard and Paulette come out into the street.

'Oh, look, there's Colin,' Pauline said, and waved.

Viv, her dress a splash of red against the black of Reg's car, turned and peered, short-sightedly, at the window.

'*There*,' Pauline said.

Colin knew Viv still couldn't see him, but she raised both arms and, enthusiastically, like somebody sending a semaphore message across a huge distance, she waved.

13

After tea, Colin got washed and changed and went down-stairs. He heard a man's voice coming from Mrs Hennigan's living room, and realized that this must be Mr Hinde. Curious to see him, this man-without-a-stomach, Colin pushed open the door, but Mr Hinde was a great disappointment. He looked just like everybody else, only thin and yellow and rather ill.

'Course you can come with us, pet,' Mrs Hennigan said. 'But are you sure you won't be bored?'

Colin was fairly sure he would be, but the prospect of an evening alone in the house frightened him. 'No, I'd like to come,' he said.

Mrs Hinde was wearing lipstick, something Colin had never known her do before, but then he'd never seen her dressed up for the spuggies. Mr Hinde's eyes followed her everywhere.

'Well, then,' Mrs Hennigan said, sticking a hat-pin through her maroon felt hat, 'Are we off?'

The spuggies held their meetings in a street of run-down, two-storey houses. Sun-blistered paint flaked from the doors, greying net curtains hung from the windows, though the house where the meeting was to be held was neater than the rest.

Prominently displayed in the bay window was a printed notice, giving the days and times of meetings. Underneath, a smaller, handwritten notice said, simply: *Female bad legs.*

Colin touched Mrs Hennigan's arm and pointed to the smaller notice. 'What's "female bad legs"?'

'It's when your varicose veins burst.' She seemed to be aware this wasn't a complete explanation, because she added, reluctantly, 'Mr Stroud used to do a lot of spiritual healing.'

'I'm surprised he's still got that notice up,' said Mr Hinde.

Stacks of hymn books stood on a table in the hall. Mrs Hennigan picked up four and handed them round. 'You're supposed to write your name on a piece of paper if you want a message,' she said, keeping her voice low.

Mr Hinde was busy writing his name.

'Every week the same,' Mrs Hinde whispered. 'And not a squeak out of her.'

'Who does he want a message from?' asked Colin.

'His first wife,' said Mrs Hinde. 'Of course I never knew the woman, but from what I can make out she was only awkward when she was here.'

Colin waited until Mr and Mrs Hinde were out of earshot, then asked, 'Was Mr Hinde very fond of his first wife?'

'No,' said Mrs Hennigan. 'He wants to know what she did with his mother's insurance money.'

They went upstairs into what had once been the main bedroom. Now it was set out as a chapel, with four or five rows of folding chairs and a table at the front. A small upright piano stood in the bay of the window.

Colin looked round and realized most of the congregation were old. Even in this weather the silence was broken by wheezing breaths and the occasional, hacking cough. He wondered if they were going to draw the curtains, and hold hands, and push that board thing round and round a table. He turned to ask Mrs Hennigan, but she was talking to Mrs Hinde.

Colin wriggled from side to side, looking at the lace curtains that shrouded the tall window. As he watched they stirred, and lacy patterns formed and shifted on the floor. The pattern lay on the creased forearm of the old lady in front of him like a tattoo.

Pierre raises the lace curtain, and peers anxiously into the street. Paulette joins him.

Maurice, the leader of the neighbouring resistance group, sits on the bed behind them. Beside him is a battered brown suitcase, containing a wireless. He's reading a notebook containing codes, and scribbling on to a pad.

PIERRE

I wish he'd get a move on.

PAULETTE

He's going as fast as he can.

She's on the verge of tears. Pierre turns from the window to look at her.

PIERRE

Hey, steady on. We'll be all right . . .

PAULETTE

Will we?

PIERRE

We've got twenty minutes. That's how long it takes them to pick up a transmission.

PAULETTE

But to do it from here!

PIERRE

We've got to contact London.

PAULETTE

It was bad luck the radio operator being killed.

PIERRE

Bad luck, was it?

Behind them Maurice pulls on the headphones, and begins to transmit.

PAULETTE

What else?

Pierre is obviously reluctant to answer.

PIERRE

Paulette, have you ever stopped to count the number of disasters there've been since Gaston arrived? The radio operator, Bernard's arrest, Antoine's son – they picked him up out of the blue, there was no sign they suspected.

PAULETTE
(*shrugging her shoulders*)
So we're having a bad run. It happens.

PIERRE

Think, Paulette.

PAULETTE

I am thinking. I'm thinking that if Gaston was a double agent, they'd've arrested us all by now.

PIERRE

Not necessarily. They might want things to go on looking normal. After all, if we were arrested some other resistance group would radio the news to London. They might not want that.

PAULETTE

Why not?

PIERRE

Because then they wouldn't be able to go on transmitting false information.

PAULETTE

You think that's what they're doing? But they can't be – you said yourself the wireless was no use without the codes.

Pierre says nothing. Simply waits.

PAULETTE
(*less certainly*)

And Gaston burnt the codebook.

PIERRE

Precisely.

They turn to watch Maurice, who's now scribbling incoming messages onto the pad.

PIERRE

You do realize, don't you, Paulette? If Gaston's lied about the codebook, he's lied about everything?

A thin, elderly woman with the beginnings of a dowager's hump came in and sat on the piano stool. Her legs were almost too short to reach the pedals, and after pumping experimentally for a minute or two, she got up and wound down the stool. At last, satisfied, she sat down again, cracked her knuckles, and started to thump out the first hymn.

The congregation, left behind despite all these preparations, struggled to their feet in an orgy of chair scraping and throat clearing. Even when, at last, they found the place in their hymn books and began to sing, their voices were, many of them, unsteady.

> *Thine be the glory, risen, conquering Son,*
> *Endless is the victory thou o'er death hast won;*
> *Angels in bright raiment rolled the stone away,*
> *Kept the folded grave clothes, where thy body lay.*

Mrs Hennigan had the only good voice in the place, a deep, rich contralto. It must have been really beautiful once, and even now it did well enough, soaring over the reedy, trembling voices of the rest.

> *Thine be the glory, risen, conquering Son,*
> *Endless is the victory thou o'er death hast won.*

The words made Colin feel sad and happy at the same time. He watched a band of sunlight creep across the floor, and remembered the open-air theatre in the park, and moved closer to Mrs Hennigan, until his sleeve was touching hers.

Half-way through the second verse, the door was flung open, and Mrs Stroud, a tall, fat woman wearing an electric blue evening dress with sequins across the bosom, entered. Behind her trotted Mr Stroud, a small, balding, sperm-shaped man.

They processed between the rows of chairs, and stood behind the table, as the congregation gathered itself to attempt the final verse.

> *No more we doubt thee, glorious Prince of Life;*
> *Life is naught without thee: aid us in our strife;*
> *Make us more than conquerers, through thy deathless love:*
> *Bring us safe through Jordan to thy home above.*

Mrs Stroud's hands were folded together in her lap like naked mice in a nest, but her eyes, pale blue and watchful, darted from face to face. When she reached Colin, her gaze lingered. He thought, as loudly as he could, *You're a fraud*, and refused to look away.

> *Thine be the glory, risen, conquering Son,*
> *Endless is the victory thou o'er death hast won.*

The congregation sat down. Nylon thighs whispered together, coughs were smothered, tummy rumbles politely ignored.

Mrs Stroud stood up and started to address the meeting. She talked a great deal about 'this vale of tears', about those who had been brought 'safe through Jordan' and were waiting to welcome us in 'that home above'.

Even in that moment of joy, she said, even in their hour of greatest triumph, they pause, they look back, they seek to comfort their loved ones, whom they have left behind on earth.

'Help us to hear them, O Lord! Help us to be like the faithful disciples. Not like Doubting Thomas . . .' Here she fixed her eyes on Colin. 'Who believed nothing till he'd *poked* his fingers into the Lord's wounds. "Blessed are they that have not seen, and yet have believed."' As she finished speaking, Mrs Stroud clasped her plump hands together, and closed her eyes.

Colin felt a quickening of expectation, as the congregation lost the slightly glazed look of people listening to a sermon, and sat further forward in their chairs, leaning towards Mrs Stroud, as if offering her their strength.

The silence deepened.

'I seem to see a man with light brown hair,' Mrs Stroud said, raising a soft, pink hand to her forehead, and speaking in a rhythmic chant. 'A young man. Wearing *blue*, a blue uniform, and he says his name's . . . *Patrick*.' Mrs Stroud opened her eyes and looked around. Shyly, blushing bright red, Mrs Hennigan raised her hand. Mrs Stroud turned in her direction, but closed her eyes again before continuing.

'He says you've been worrying a lot about a young man, a young man with fair hair.'

'Yes,' said Mrs Hennigan.

'And this young man's been led astray in the past, hasn't he, by a false friend? A dark man. Dark in feature, dark in nature.' She clutched her forehead with both hands. 'I see a tall building with bars.'

Abruptly, she opened her eyes and addressed Mrs Hennigan in a more normal voice. 'Patrick says you've got to stop worrying, love. He says, You've got to remember he's a man now, and it's up to him what he does with his life, and it's no use you fretting yourself sick about it, because that's what you have been doing, isn't it? You've just got to have faith. Young people make mistakes, but they sort themselves out in the end, and it's not a bit of good you trying to solve the problems for him — he's got to do that himself.'

Mrs Hennigan was sobbing, long before the end of this speech. Colin watched her out of the corner of his eye, and at last put his hand on her arm. 'I'm all right, flower,' she said, smiling and sniffing. 'It's wonderful what she sees, isn't it?'

Next, Mrs Stroud announced the presence of a tall, dark man, heavily built, with a high colour. '*Very* big built, he is,' she said. 'With a terrible cough. He says his name's . . .'

'George!' cried a woman in the front row.

'*George.*' Mrs Stroud listened, and moaned. 'Oh-oh.'

'What's the matter?'

'George can't rest,' said Mrs Stroud. 'He says he went up there for a bit of peace and he's had none since he got there.' She listened again. 'He says he can't rest because he knows you're unhappy. He says you've been offered the chance of happiness, and he says, "Flo," he says . . . Is it Flo?'

'Yes.'

'"Take it," he says. "Seize it with both hands. If you're happy," he says, "I'm happy."' Mrs Stroud opened her eyes, and said gently, 'You know, love, it's been a long time. George wants to sleep now.'

Flo was looking puzzled.

'What is it, dear?'

'Has he still got that cough?'

Mrs Stroud took a deep breath. 'No, dear. As I think I've explained before, the astral body is perfect. George *mentioned* his cough, because he knew that would bring him back to you.'

Mrs Stroud sank back into her chair, exhausted. Mr Stroud stood up and announced, with more animation than he'd yet shown, that a collection would be taken during the singing of the next hymn.

After the collection – whose progress from row to row Mr Stroud watched intently – Mrs Stroud stood up again and began to describe 'spirit visitors' who, she said, were standing behind the chairs of people in the room. Most of the invisible guests turned out to be white-haired and very old, and all were joyfully claimed by their white-haired, elderly sons and daughters.

This pattern went on unchanged, until she reached Mr Hinde. 'I see a Red Indian,' she said. 'He's got long grey hair, iron-grey – down to his shoulders, and a band tied round his head. Oh and he's got an eagle feather stuck through the band. He says he doesn't want to give his name . . .'

He didn't need to, Colin thought. It was Jeff Chandler in *Broken Arrow*.

'. . . but he sends fraternal greetings, and says, "Keep drinking the milk".'

Colin was next. Mrs Stroud smiled at him, a distinctly sickly smile, and began, 'I see . . .'

What she was going to pretend to see Colin never found out, because the next word stuck in her throat. She put a hand up, as if to clear the blockage, and tried to go on speaking, but no words came out. Her eyes were fixed on a point behind Colin's chair.

Colin gazed straight ahead, resisting the temptation to look around, though the hairs on the nape of his neck crawled.

After a while, Mrs Stroud seemed to relax, and crumple at the same time. She fell back against the table, scattering a pile of leaflets onto the floor. Mr Stroud stared at her in badly-disguised amazement, but recovered himself quickly, and announced, 'We shall now sing hymn number ninety-four, "Guide me, O Thou Great Jehovah . . ."'

The congregation struggled to its feet, disturbed by the change in routine. For the first time that evening, Colin thought, their faith had been shaken. Mrs Stroud's collapse looked like fraud, to those who were accustomed to her chantings and moanings; though no fraud could have produced the sweat that melted her make-up, or have given to the pale eyes and slightly prominent teeth the glazed look of a dying rabbit.

> Guide me, O thou great Jehovah,
>   Pilgrim through this barren land;
> I am weak, but thou art mighty,
>   Hold me with thy powerful hand;
>   Bread of heaven,
>   Bread of heaven,
> Feed me till I want no more.
> Feed me till I want no more.

The singing was ragged, and more than once the piano wavered as the pianist turned to look over her shoulder at Mrs Stroud. Neither of the Strouds made any attempt to join in the singing. Mrs Hennigan took over, throwing her voice across the room, establishing the tune, rallying the waverers. The noise became at first respectable and then thunderous.

> Death of Death, and Hell's destruction
> Land me safe on Canaan's side.
>   Songs and praises
>   Songs and praises

I will ever give to thee.
I will ever give to thee.

After a short closing prayer, the congregation filed out, their whispers creating a troubled hum sufficiently unlike the usual noise to cause Mr Stroud's eyes to dart from face to face. Mrs Stroud's colour was beginning to come back.

Out in the hall, Mr Hinde, who seemed to be unaware that anything unusual had happened, said, in his usual complaining voice, 'She keeps giving me that Red Indian. I don't know any Red Indians.'

'Perhaps it's your spirit guide,' Mrs Hennigan said.

'Some guide. *"Keep drinking the milk."* It's not as if I can drink anything else.'

They were just about to leave when Mrs Stroud appeared on the stairs. She and Mrs Hennigan spoke together. Colin waited in the porch, not expecting any share of the conversation, but then he heard his name.

'Colin,' Mrs Hennigan said.

He went back into the hall to join them.

Mrs Stroud's hands were cuddling each other again. 'I was just saying to Mrs Hennigan, I wouldn't mind having a chat with that young man.'

Mrs Hennigan hesitated. 'Well, what do you think, Colin? Would you like to stay and have a chat?'

Colin was surprised at how clear and definite his voice sounded. 'Yes,' he said. 'Yes, I would.'

14

They went along the passage and down the steps into the basement kitchen. Plastic curtains, with a pattern of looped daisies, shrouded the window, letting in a mingy light. Mr Stroud and the lady who had played the piano were nowhere to be seen.

'Sit yourself down, son,' Mrs Stroud said. 'We just might have some orange juice.'

It didn't seem likely. A bottle of gin, half empty, stood on the draining board. Beside it, in the soap dish, sat a cake of Lifebuoy toilet soap, cracked, and flaking at the edges. Apart from these the kitchen looked remarkably bare.

Colin sat at the table. It was covered with a plastic cloth, in the same pattern of looped daisies as the curtains. Here and there, bubbles of air had got trapped beneath, and Colin passed the time squeezing them surreptitiously to the edge of the
cloth.

'Here we are,' Mrs Stroud said.

She produced a bottle of lemonade from inside a cupboard at the end of the room, and poured Colin a glass. Colin sipped the flattest lemonade he'd ever tasted, and watched as Mrs Stroud poured herself a tumbler of gin.

'There now,' she said, and sat down beside him.

Close to, she looked a bit bedraggled. The sequins on her bosom continued to flash blue fire, but here and there they'd moulted, leaving patches of bald chiffon, through which a great deal of pink flesh showed.

'You live with Mrs Hennigan, don't you?'

'Yes.'

'I've known her years. I was the barmaid at the Black Swan during the war, and she used to come in the mornings and clean. She used to bring their Adrian and leave him in the back room while she worked. Oh, and what a lovely kid. But spoilt. Right from the start she spoilt him, but after his dad died she turned him into a little tin god. Oh, I know them well.'

'You know them all, don't you?'

'Yes, son, I know them all. It's very rare anybody walks through the door I can't put a name to, and if I can't it's ten to one Mr Stroud can.' She smiled. 'Don't you worry, I had you spotted for a clever-clogs the minute you walked in. You were a lot of bother to me in that meeting, young man.'

'Sorry . . .'

'No need.' She waved her gin in token of forgiveness. 'It's just some things are only possible in the presence of great faith. Miracles are one, and fraud's another.'

Colin was shocked. *He* knew she was a fraud, but he didn't think it was right for her to say so.

'You know that woman I give the message to from George?'

'Yes.'

'Well, George died of a heart attack. Big fella, smoked like a chimney, nobody could tell him anything, but he was a good husband, for all that. They were like this.' Mrs Stroud crossed two fingers. 'Never had no kids, it was just her and him and the bloody budgie . . . And the consequence was, she was lost when he went. Absolutely lost. You believe me, if she'd moped any more she'd've followed him. Well, last November, her sister talked her into going to the tombola. "Oh, I don't feel like it," she says, "me nerves are bad." "Shurrup about your nerves," she says. "You're going." Well, anyway, she went, and she got on with this fella, and ever since then she's been tormenting herself. You know, she thinks if she fancies another bloke it means she didn't really love George, and all that kind of rubbish. So anyway, I thought it was time George put in a word. No harm in that, is there?'

'No.'

'I notice she put a shilling in the collection. I reckon she got a bloody good bobsworth.'

'And Mr Hinde?'

'Oh, him and his insurance money. How the hell am I supposed to know what she did with it? She was a heavy drinker. You don't ask where money goes when you've got one of them in the house.' She refilled her glass. 'So who is he, then?'

'Who?'

'*Who.* Your little friend you brought in with you.'

'I don't know what you saw.'

'Oh, out comes the finger, *poke, poke, poke.* I'm serious, you know, I'm going to call you Thomas.' Her eyes hardened. 'I saw a tall, thin, fair-haired man in a black coat. Looked as if he'd lost a quid and found a penny.'

'I don't know anybody who looks like that.'

'You mean you've never seen him?'

'No.' Colin hadn't intended to lie, but, sitting there, his skin sticking to sweaty plastic, he felt suddenly that any admission would give the thing – whatever it was – greater reality. 'No, I can't place him at all.'

Mrs Stroud laughed. 'You'll have to lie better than that if you want to fool me.'

Her voice was sharp. She seemed to make no concessions at all to Colin's age. Normally he would have liked that, but today it frightened him. She was treating him as an equal, because of that thing behind his chair.

'Well, he gave me a nasty turn. It's been years since anything like that happened to me.'

'Oh, so it has happened before?'

He knew he sounded too eager, and looked down to avoid her glance.

'Regular occurrence, once,' she said. 'Oh, I know you think I'm a fraud, and I don't deny it, but it wasn't always like that. I had the gift. And the funny thing was I didn't realize it till quite late on. I was brought up as a Baptist, you see. It was the war got me into spiritualism. I knew all the lads up at the aerodrome, the Swan was their local. You'd talk to them one evening, they'd be laughing and joking on, and the next day they were dead. I remember one morning I walked into the pub and there was this lad sat on a stool by the bar. I says, "Hey, we're not open." Oh, and he turned round, and he looked at me and I knew straight away. I thought, "Well. He never hurt you when he was alive, he's not going to hurt you now." So I just says, "Welcome home, son." And after that I used to see them often. Young souls, you see. No warning. They're bewildered. And then I started coming to the meetings here and then was when I met Mr Stroud. And then after a while he says, "You know, you should be taking these meetings." I says, "*No.*" "*Yes,*" he says. "You've got the gift." And I had, Colin. *I had.*'

She leant towards him. He caught her smell, a smell of talcum powder, and gin and sweat, and looked away.

'But the trouble is, you see, the meetings come round twice a week, and you can't just switch that power on when you want it. Sometimes your mind's a blank, you've nothing to tell them, but they're still sat there. And you can see in their faces what they *want* to be told. And so you start to tell them that. You pretend it's there when it isn't. And then, gradually, the real thing happens less and less often, and you fake it more and more, until in the end it's all fake.'

'And the healing?'

'That was Mr Stroud's . . . sideline. People are very ready to see wrong where none exists.'

Mrs Stroud lapsed into silence. Colin began to think she'd forgotten he was there, but then she said, '*You*'ve got the gift.'

'*No*,' said Colin.

'Yes, you have. I was watching you, you knew what was behind that chair as well as I did.' She leant forward. 'You've got to take care of it, Colin. Don't let it slip away, don't do what I did. You can use it to make yourself look good, you can use it to get even with people, but I'm warning you, if you do, you'll lose it. And it won't just go away and leave you in peace, either. It isn't like that.' She tapped her sequined bosom with one podgy hand. 'It stays in *here* and it rots.'

Colin was beginning to be afraid. Not of Mrs Stroud, for clearly she meant him no harm, but of the future, of the possibility, suddenly glimpsed, that *his* life might end like this. Like most young people, he'd always assumed, without ever really thinking about it, that regret, waste, failure lay in wait for others, but not for him. Now, squeezing bubbles of air to the edge of Mrs Stroud's tablecloth, he realized, for the first time, that he was not exempt, that this, unless he took steps to avoid it, could happen to him.

He ought to have left then, but he didn't. He stayed, while Mrs Stroud became drunker and more despairing, more slurred in her speech, more unsteady in her movements, until at last Mr Stroud, the spiritual healer of female bad legs, appeared in the doorway, and said, 'My God. Pissed again.' He crossed to the table, picked up the empty bottle and, not looking at Colin, said, 'I think you'd better go.'

Colin tiptoed along the corridor and out of the house, feeling, as he ran across the street into the sunshine, that he was escaping from a dark cave.

15

The way to Ross's house led across a bombed site. Houses had been blown up or demolished, and a cross-section cut through the body of the street. At one side a mantelpiece jutted into nothing; at the other, the fading pattern of roses on a wall was broken by a lighter square, where once a picture had hung.

In the gap between, a wilderness grew. Bracken, bramble, ragwort, coltsfoot, nettles, vetch, ragged robin, dandelion, rosebay – a green labyrinth, baking in the heat. Insects droned obsessively, drunken bees fumbled from flower to flower, and the sun, slipping down behind the roofs of the still-intact houses opposite, etched individual leaves and stems in gold.

Colin stopped at his favourite place, a bomb-crater that, unlike all the others, had not been filled in. He scrambled down the slope, dislodging small stones that peppered after him, and sat with his back against a rusty pram, his face upturned to the fading sun.

All around him was the smell of dusty nettles, and when he opened his eyes he saw a ladybird, half-hidden in the curl of a leaf. But he was aware of other life here, life you couldn't see, small animals that darted and burrowed, birds that peered down through open rafters, surveying the desolation with unblinking, golden eyes.

Behind the lace curtains, Pierre and Paulette watch as Maurice finishes decoding the message and turns to them.

MAURICE
There was a two-day break in transmissions. Then they started again.

Paulette looks at Pierre, even now not wanting to believe what she's been told.

Apparently, he said he'd fallen off his bike and broken his wrist. Very neat. Explained why the rhythm had changed.

PIERRE
(*deep, gasping breath*)
That's that, then.

PAULETTE
I suppose there could be some other explanation . . .

PIERRE
Gaston swore he destroyed that codebook. If the Germans have it, it's because he gave it to them.

Maurice begins to pack the wireless back into the case.

PAULETTE
What are we going to do?

PIERRE

What we always do.

PAULETTE

No, Pierre. He's only a boy . . .

PIERRE

Age has nothing to do with it. You know that perfectly well.

MAURICE

He's right, Paulette.

He clicks the suitcase shut.

I suggest we leave separately. If you need me again, Pierre, you know where to contact me.

He opens the door, listens, and then slips away down the stairs. Through the lace curtains they watch him cross the street and walk away.

PIERRE

Where is Gaston now?

PAULETTE

He said he was going to the safe house to check on Bernard.

She says this almost casually, letting the lace curtain drop. Then she realizes what she's said and looks at Pierre.

PIERRE

Oh my God.

Mark stood naked between Mr Williams's knees. He turned as Colin came in, his dark eyes filmed with tiredness.

'Sit yourself down,' Mr Williams said. 'Ross won't be a minute.'

Mark went on staring at Colin, until his father pulled him round and dried his face, dabbing the fluffy towel on the end of his nose until he giggled. Then he lifted him out of the water, and began to dry his legs, the child standing first on one foot and then the other, resting his square, podgy hands on his father's knees.

When he was dry, Mr Williams lifted the bowl and carried it through into the kitchen. Left alone with Colin, Mark seemed more alarmed than curious. He ran out after his father. 'What's the matter with you?' Colin heard Mr Williams say. 'You've seen Colin before.'

Ross came into the room. 'Oh, hi, Colin.'

'Are you coming out?'

Mr Williams came back into the room, drying his arms on a towel.

'Can I, Dad?'

'Aye, go on. But don't you be late back, mind. And *don't* play on that bomb-site.'

The bomb-site was forbidden because the houses on either side of it were supposed to be dangerous. In spite of that, or perhaps because of it, it had long been the favourite meeting place of the gang.

They didn't need to consult each other. They went straight there.

Gradually, as the evening wore on, the rocking air, the blast, the shattered windows, the cries, came to seem more real than the green world they tunnelled through to reach their targets. They were by turns bomber pilots, clasped hands simulating RT masks as they made Dambuster-type approaches to a broken bedstead; and victims, rolling on the ground and screaming, until at last they came to rest, looking up at the dark heads of nettles outlined against the sky.

Moonlight, draining the world of colour, transformed the bomb-site into the kind of ruin Colin remembered from photographs. Weeds still formed a blurred and shifting foreground, but it was the background you noticed now: the jagged edges of broken walls, doors that opened into nothing.

They left the bomb-site, and started to play in the houses that surrounded it. These were boarded up, but it made no difference. A sheet of corrugated iron swung out, and a living-room window became a door.

'Careful,' Colin whispered, as Ross crawled in. But he didn't mean the rotting floorboards, or the ceilings that sagged and dribbled plaster down the walls. He meant the Germans, who had a machine-gun sited in the front bedroom window.

They crept upstairs. As their heads drew level with the landing, they peered through the banisters. The back bedroom was empty. Colin nodded to Ross and began to sidle along the landing towards the front room. Outside the door he stopped, flicked his tongue once over dry lips, and exploded into the room.

His first, crazy, split-second thought was that the moon had somehow got into the house, for there, in front of him, was a white, round, gleaming, globular, spherical object, moving up and down in the darkness. Another second, and he knew it was a bum.

He backed away, and collided with Ross, who chose that moment to leap, gun-centred, into the room.

'Aaagh!' cried Ross.

'Aaagh!' cried the owner of the bum.

He was unwinding himself, and turning at the same time, climbing to what seemed to Colin a great height. A pink knob, shrinking rapidly, bobbed gently in a nest of black hair. Colin lifted his eyes to the face.

And then he ran, pushing Ross ahead of him down the stairs. They scrambled out of the window, and stopped to listen, but heard only the murmur of voices.

Silently, not looking at each other, they replaced the corrugated iron sheet.

They were subdued on the way home. At first they didn't speak at all, but then Colin said, 'You know who that was, don't you?'

'Yeh,' said Ross.

They went on a little further. Colin was thinking back over what he'd seen, trying to fix his vague impression of the woman. He felt quite vicious towards her, he didn't know why. 'Did you see *her*?' he said. 'She was a right old ratbag. You'd think he could do better than that.'

'You get pretty desperate in prison,' Ross said, seriously.

And suddenly, looking at the corner of Ross's mouth, Colin knew it wasn't serious at all, it was funny. He started to laugh, and nudged Ross, determined to make him laugh too. He jerked his pelvis, imitating the movements of the moon-bum, and at last Ross started to giggle.

Soon they were whirling along the street, chanting a song Colin made up as they went:

> *We saw*
> *Combey's bum.*
> *He hadn't got*
> *His trousers on.*

> *We saw*
> *Combey's dick.*
> *What a sight,*
> *Made you sick.*

> *We saw*
> *Combey's balls . . .*

Two middle-aged ladies, walking home, smiled at this display of childish exuberance, though their expressions changed when they heard the words. Ross nudged Colin, who abruptly stopped singing. This was Ross's street.

They walked on, more soberly now, though bubbles of laughter still burst on the surface now and then, until they reached Ross's door.

It began to rain, as Colin left Ross's street and turned into Clifford Avenue, a heavy downpour that washed the dust from the leaves and restored the green smell of early summer. Colin didn't hurry. He rather liked rain, especially summer rain. Pavements gleamed, streetlamps blossomed, cars passed in a slush and whisper of tyres.

A sleek, powerful black car with its windscreen wipers swishing, pulls into the kerb. Switching off the engine, the Kommandant turns to Vivienne.

KOMMANDANT

I won't be a moment, my dear. I just have to deliver these files.

After he's gone Vivienne opens her powder compact and checks her lipstick, using her index finger to remove a tiny smear from below her lower lip. She moves the mirror further up, and begins shaping her fringe. Suddenly she looks puzzled, she's seen something she doesn't understand reflected in the glass. She closes the compact and leans over to peer through the rain-flawed window.

Gaston is leaving Gestapo headquarters by the same side entrance that the Kommandant has just used. Bewildered, Vivienne puts her hand on the handle of the door and seems about to open it and call his name, but then she draws back.

She sits facing forward again, enclosed, almost it seems imprisoned, by the pelting of rain onto the car roof.

*

Rain rattled against Colin's bedroom window. For once he'd closed the curtains, because he didn't want to lie and wait for the trawl of light across the ceiling. Though when, at last, he heard the car, he went and stood on the landing, looking down through the banisters.

Viv came in first. She put a finger to her lips, but Reg pushed it aside and started kissing her. His right hand slid down her back, and felt her bottom, then moved to her thigh and began rucking up her skirt till the stocking tops showed. She pushed him away, but only to laugh, and clasp his hand, and pull him up the stairs behind her.

Colin retreated into his bedroom, and shut the door. He lay on the bed, hearing their whispers, the rustle and click of clothes going off, and then the clanging and creaking of springs. After a while, he rolled over onto his stomach and pulled the pillow over his head, so that he didn't have to hear any more.

Involuntarily – like the tide sweeping into a rock-pool – his mind filled with images of clutching hands and heaving bottoms. He tried to keep his mind away from what was happening next door, to fix it on Combey and the woman in the bombed house. Again he imitated the thrust of Combey's pelvis, but this time it wasn't funny. He felt himself swell and stiffen, his breath caught in his throat, and then, all at once, the tension was bursting and flowing out of him.

When it stopped, and he could be still again, he turned on his side, and stared at the wall. Using its whiteness as a screen, he flicked back through the images, and knew that in the end it hadn't been Combey and the unknown woman he'd been thinking about.

He began to rub himself dry on the sheet, feeling small, grubby and alone.

*

Pierre, followed by Paulette, is climbing the narrow staircase towards the top flat of the safe house, where Bernard is hiding. He taps cautiously on the door. No answer. He looks at Paulette.

PAULETTE

Perhaps he's gone out.

PIERRE

No, he couldn't risk doing that. Bernard?

PAULETTE
(*nervously*)
If they've got him, they'll be watching the house.

PIERRE

They don't need to watch anything, my dear. They know all about us, remember? I'm going to force the lock.

He takes a run at the door. The lock breaks and he bursts into the room, followed by Paulette. Bernard, still wearing the red dress, lies on his stomach on the bed, his face turned towards the door, but hidden by the long blonde hair of his wig.

PAULETTE

Bernard.

She goes across and reaches out to touch his shoulder.

PIERRE

Too late.

PAULETTE

Oh, Bernard.

She brushes the hair back from the dead face. And then steps back, gasping with shock, for the body on the bed is not Bernard, after all, but Vivienne.

Saturday

16

Colin woke to a hot bed, and sunlight that hurt his eyes. He twisted round to look at his arm, and saw that the marks – the fingerprints – had joined together to form a big, raised, angry patch.

He lay and watched a blade of sunlight edge across the floor, wondering if he wanted a glass of water badly enough to get up and get it.

Something was niggling him, something he'd dreamt, perhaps. And then he remembered – Viv was dead. No, not dead, he'd *dreamt* she was dead. Or imagined she was dead. It was difficult to keep things clear.

The silence in the next room became threatening. How could you be sure a dream was just a dream? He listened, waiting for the creak of bedsprings as she turned, but it never came. At last, telling himself he was being stupid, he got up, padded onto the landing in his bare feet, and listened.

Nothing.

Unable to bear the fear any longer, he pushed the door open and looked in.

Viv lay curled up in bed, her blonde hair covering her face. Beside her, beginning to wake up, and mutter, and make goldfish movements with his lips, was Mr Boyce. Viv groaned, pushing the hair out of her eyes. 'Colin? What do you *want*?'

'Glass of water.'

'Well, you won't find it in here.'

Well, at least she was alive, Colin thought. He poured himself a glass of water and drank it slowly, seeing, in his mind's eye, the blonde head and the dark head side by side. Mr Boyce had never stayed the whole night before. Perhaps it meant he was getting serious? Perhaps he was thinking of leaving his wife and moving in here?

Colin refilled the glass, carried it into his bedroom, and set it down on the bedside table.

I don't want that to happen, he thought.

When Colin finally gave up trying to sleep and went downstairs, he found Mr Boyce standing in the bay window, looking out into the street. He turned as Colin came in. 'Hello, son.'

Poking my mother does not give you the right to call me 'son'. ''Lo.'

Colin knelt on the clip mat and started to clear the grate, more to give himself something to do than because a fire was needed.

'Bit hot for that, isn't it, son?'

'I'm not lighting it. I'm laying it.'

Viv came into the room, wearing only her slip. 'Do you think we need that, Colin?'

Colin took a deep breath. 'I'm not lighting it. I'm laying it.'

Viv reached up to get a blouse from the airing rack above the fireplace. Colin smelled her warm skin through the nylon slip, and heard the slight rasp as her stocking tops rubbed together. 'Do you mind, Mam?' he said, elbowing her away.

He felt them exchange glances over his head.

'I'll just get the kettle on,' Viv said. 'Tea or coffee?'

'Tea, please.'

'Colin?'

'Tea.'

Viv went into the kitchen. Mr Boyce looked at Colin and Colin looked back.

'I thought we might have a run down the coast later on,' Mr Boyce said. 'The three of us.'

Viv called from the kitchen. 'Yes, isn't that nice, Colin?'

'I'm afraid I can't,' Colin said.

'Why not?' asked Viv, bouncing back into the room.

'I'm playing football for the school.'

Mr Boyce smiled. 'Oh, you're in the school team, are you?'

'Yes.' He added, reluctantly, 'It's the first practice.'

'Well,' said Mr Boyce. 'We certainly can't ask him to miss that.'

He was relieved, even if Viv wasn't.

'One thing you always want to remember, son. It's not *what* you know in this life, it's *who* you know. And you'll get to know more people on a football pitch than you ever will with your nose stuck in a book.'

'Aw, what a shame,' Viv said. 'I was looking forward to that.'

'*You* can still go,' Colin said.

'I'll have to go home first,' Mr Boyce said. 'You know, Marion might . . .'

'Yes,' said Viv, quickly, with a glance at Colin.

'But I should be back by half ten. Eleven at the latest.'

Viv returned to the kitchen. Colin stared at Mr Boyce, turning him first into the Kommandant – brutal, blue eyes, skin the colour of pork sausages – and then into a spiv with slickly Brylcreemed hair, shielding a cigarette in his cupped hand, jacket pulled out of shape by dozens of black market nylons. *That* was more *his* style.

Mr Boyce, unaware of the transformations he'd just undergone, but made nervous by Colin's scrutiny, smiled, and started to say something about the value of team games in the formation of character.

Colin made himself listen, and even responded. They talked about football and when that subject was exhausted they talked about cars. All the while Colin was wondering how to get rid of him. No point saying anything rude. Whenever he did that, Mr Boyce looked at him with a tolerant and understanding expression. *Brought up without a father*, he seemed to be saying. *What else can you expect?*

And suddenly Colin knew what to do.

'You know me mam and me were on talking the other day. About what I ought to call you.'

'Ye-es?'

'Well, you know, "Mr Boyce" sounds a bit stand-offish, doesn't it? So me mam was saying she thought I ought to call you Uncle Reg.'

'Good idea,' said Mr Boyce, without a great deal of enthusiasm.

'I said, why don't I call him "Dad"?'

Mr Boyce seemed a little startled, as if, Colin thought, somebody had just rammed an electric cattle prod up his arse.

'But me mam says, "No, Colin, it's a bit early for that". She says, "I know it means a lot to you, son, but believe me it's better to wait till we're living together." '

'*She said that?*'

'Yes,' said Colin. 'And I could see the sense of it. So that's what we agreed, *Uncle Reg*.'

'I'll leave you two with the teapot,' Viv said, coming back into the room. 'I'll have to go upstairs and get ready.'

Mr Boyce stood up. 'No, well, actually, love, I think I'd better be going.'

'Oh,' Viv said. 'Surely you've got time for a cup of tea . . .'

He took her by the shoulders. 'The sooner I go the sooner I'll be back.'

'All right, then.'

He bent and kissed her, but busily, as if the kiss were one of a series of jobs.

'Eleven o'clock, then?'

'Yes.'

They heard him clatter down the stairs. Viv went to the bay window to watch him drive away, but though her hand was half-raised, ready to wave, he didn't look back.

Viv's handbag, with a pair of short, white gloves folded across it, lay ready on the table by the door.

Viv herself was sitting in the armchair, buffing her finger-nails, holding them out at arm's length to admire the result. Colin hated her for being so eager, so thrilled at the prospect of a day out, so *available*. Then he remembered how her clothes smelled of chicken fat when she came in from the club.

'You'll wear your fingernails out,' he said.

She looked up and smiled. 'How's it going?'

'OK.'

Colin had spread newspaper over the kitchen table, and was working on his model aeroplanes. Several of them stood around in varying stages of completion. At the moment, he was cutting out balsawood struts for a Spitfire, the light from the window glinting on the blade of his knife.

'I wonder what made Reg rush off like that?' Viv said. 'I

thought he'd've stayed for his breakfast. He didn't say anything, did he, while I was in the kitchen?'

'Only that he had to get back in case there was a call. He seemed a bit worried about it.'

'Oh well.' A forced smile. 'Are you going to the pictures?'

'No, not today. I thought I'd give it a miss. I don't feel so good.'

She got up and came across to the table. 'No, and you don't look it. C'mon, let's have a look at that arm.'

Reluctantly, Colin rolled up his sleeve. The last thing he wanted, at that moment, was kindness from Viv.

'Aw, Colin, you can't play football with that.'

'I play football with me feet.'

She put a hand to his forehead. 'You're hot. Why don't you go and have a lie down?'

'Because I want to finish this.'

He put the Spitfire to one side, and began to dope a Hurricane. As the skin wrinkled and sagged, the room filled with the smell of peardrops. Colin raised his fingers to his nostrils, and breathed deeply, watching Viv watch the clock.

In the other kitchen, Pierre is pacing up and down. It's clear from his pale skin and shadowed eyes that he hasn't managed to get much sleep. Paulette is sitting at the table surrounded by the remains of breakfast.

PIERRE

Why do it? Why destroy her like that?

PAULETTE

Perhaps he mistook her for Bernard.

PIERRE

No, he knew what he was doing. He must've been looking straight at her when he did it. But *why*?

I think she saw something, something she didn't understand, and went to tell Bernard. And he realized what it meant, swapped clothes with her, and moved on.

Leaving her to face Gaston? I don't believe it.

No. No, I think that was her idea. She'd want to give Gaston a chance to explain. She was always very fond of him, you know. In her way.

Colin was painting a Lysander. Brown and green on top to merge into the countryside, grey and white underneath to fade into the sky. When it was done, he sat back and looked at it, rubbing the skin of dry paint that had formed over the tip of his index finger.

'I can't think what's keeping him,' Viv said.

'Perhaps his wife's showed up.'

'No, I don't think so. He seemed pretty definite she was going for the weekend.' She looked at the clock. 'I'll give it another half hour.'

It was already half past eleven. Colin picked up the Lysander, and fled.

On the back step he stopped, and, fingers splayed, thumb covering the sun, he searched the sky for enemy planes. When no menacing specks appeared, he lifted the Lysander and launched it.

It glided sharply down, and seemed at first to be heading straight for the lawn, but then a gust of wind seized it, and bore it triumphantly aloft. High above the shed roof it soared and Colin, afraid of losing it altogether, started to chase it down the garden, but then, abruptly, it lost height, and crashed into the elder tree, where it hung, dipping slightly as the branches swayed.

Colin jumped up, trying to shake the Lysander free, but he couldn't reach. He'd given up and was looking round for a stick, when Adrian came out of the shed. He was stripped to the waist, and wearing the jeans he always wore when working on his bike.

'Hang on, I'll get it.' He stretched to his full height, revealing a band of white skin below the belt of his jeans. "S not bad that,' he said, examining the plane. 'Go on, give it another go.'

Colin ran back to the top of the steps, and launched the plane. Adrian, slowly wiping his hands on a piece of oil-stained rag, watched from the end of the lawn. The plane swooped down, and landed almost at his feet.

He watched a couple more flights, none of them particularly successful, then drifted back into the shed.

Colin decided to give it one more go. Infuriatingly, now that Adrian wasn't there to watch, the Lysander flew the whole length of the garden, and landed in the long grass behind the shed.

Colin had picked it up and was examining it for signs of damage, when he heard a sound behind him, and spun round. A hideous face, with a long snout, and huge discs for eyes, thrust itself into his own.

He realized, almost at once, that it was Adrian, wearing one of the gas masks that hung from a nail in the shed. Colin had often played with them himself, when he was younger, he and Ross chasing each other round and round the house. Even now he remembered the rubbery smell, the way the cheek parts, sucked in and out with every breath, were always cold against your skin.

'Adrian, stop it.' His voice sounded sharper, more alarmed, than he thought he felt. 'Don't be so daft.'

But Adrian wouldn't stop. He darted towards Colin, arms

angled away from his body, moving like a spider, a hunting spider, in crabbed rushes and starts.

Colin began to dodge, always being forced back towards the shed, and always resisting the temptation to hide inside it. Once in there he was trapped.

He feinted towards the door. Adrian lunged, leaving a gap that Colin managed to wriggle through. He ran across the lawn and up the steps, three at a time, bursting into the passage, where he tripped and almost fell, for after the brightness of the garden, the house seemed black, totally black, and cold.

He groped his way down the passage to the foot of the stairs, and there stopped, unwilling to go upstairs and face Viv again. Instead, he slipped into Adrian's room, and closed the door.

He stood behind it, breathing quietly, listening for the pad of footsteps. They came closer, hesitated, and stopped.

The doorhandle began to turn, and then the door swung open. The long snout and huge eyes emerged from the darkness of the passage, and came towards him. And suddenly Colin knew it wasn't Adrian, at all, but something else, something terrible, something so entirely alien that its face, revealed, would be more dreadful than the mask.

Colin backed away, and the thing followed. The ground seemed to be shifting, to be falling away beneath him, and then, as the cold rubber touched his skin, as the arms reached out and seized him, his knees buckled, and he fell.

17

When Colin opened his eyes, he knew at once by the position of the window that he was in his own room, and in bed. Feeling hot and sticky, he poked his head out of the bedclothes. A face loomed towards him, the metal rims of its glasses glinting like knives.

'Well, young man, we are in a pickle, aren't we?'

Colin tried to sit up. The sheets felt hot and clammy against his skin.

'Are you hot?'

'Boiling.'

The man produced a thermometer and Colin opened his

mouth to take it. Somewhere out of sight a floorboard creaked. While Colin held the thermometer under his tongue, the doctor examined his arm, lingering over the red patch. Colin tried to remember what had happened, but could recall nothing, except the cold feel of the snout against his skin. He must have fainted, he supposed, though he didn't feel faint now. Only hot.

The doctor took the thermometer from his mouth, and read it.

'103,' he said, looking over his shoulder. He turned back to Colin. 'Open.' He shone a torch into Colin's mouth, twisted his head this way and that, pressed his fingers into the sides of his neck. 'Well, the throat's a bit red, but that's all. Better keep him in bed. And no school Monday.' He twinkled at Colin. 'That's the good news, isn't it?'

The floorboards creaked again. Colin could hear Viv and the doctor whispering together on the landing. Then the murmur of a hand sliding down the banister. He tried to sit up, but he didn't have the energy.

The door opened, and he realized Viv must have come back into the room. He lay there, waiting for her to speak. Then came a sound so dry, so difficult, that at first he couldn't think what it was. As he struggled to sit up, the sounds combined into a steady sobbing.

'Mam.'

Viv gulped and blew her nose.

'Mam, I'm sorry.'

'What you got to be sorry about?' She sniffed. ''S not your fault you're ill.'

'No, I meant Reg.'

She shrugged. 'I really pick 'em, don't I? Still, it's probably just as well. I couldn't go out and leave you like this.'

Colin turned restlessly. 'I'm hot.'

'I know, son. I'll just go and get a couple of aspirin, see if that brings it down.' She came across to the bed and straightened the quilt. 'There's nowt worse than a temperature for making you feel rotten. I remember once I thought I was a cockroach. I could hear me wings rubbing together and everything.'

Colin smiled, but he didn't really think it was funny. The way he felt at the moment, turning into a cockroach seemed only too probable.

'Adrian's downstairs. Having kittens. I think he thinks he's killed you. Have I to send him up?'

Adrian came in, looking sheepish.

'Hello, Col, you all right?'

'Oh, not so bad. Wasn't your fault, you know. I've been feeling a bit off all morning.'

'What did the doctor say?'

'Stop in bed.' He grinned. 'Stop off school.'

'Oh, so it's not all bad. I wish somebody'd tell me to stop off work.'

'Aw, go on, you love it.'

Adrian couldn't sit on the bed because of the oil on his jeans. Instead he half-knelt, half-squatted, on the floor.

'Brought your plane back,' he said. 'Have I to hang it up for you?'

'Aye, go on. Look, there's a nail.'

Adrian attached a length of white thread to the plane, and tied it to the nail, where it floated gently in the draught from the open window. 'There, looks good, that.'

Colin would have liked to mention Brian, but he didn't know how. He wondered whether Adrian knew the woman Brian had been with, or whether it was just somebody Brian had picked up. Whether Brian would tell Adrian about it, or keep it a secret.

There was quite a lot he didn't know, and wanted to know, and couldn't find out, because everybody pretended it didn't happen. Whereas you knew perfectly well that night after night hundreds of thousands of men, *millions*, climbed on top of women, and stuck their things into a hole between their legs, and waggled them in and out. He knew that one day this would seem unsurprising, but it didn't seem unsurprising now. He was *amazed*.

'Saw Brian last night.'

'Did you?'

'Yeh. He was with a lass.'

Lass. She was thirty if she was a day.

'Dark-haired lass? Yeh, we bumped into her in the Feathers.' Adrian gave the Lysander a little push and set it swinging. 'Don't know what he got up to in prison, but it didn't half ruin his eyesight.'

'Nah, she wasn't much.'

Adrian smiled, the way grown-ups did when you said something grown up. He minded when Adrian did it, because when they'd first met, Adrian had been almost within reach. Well, still at school.

'You like Brian, don't you?' he said.

'We go back a long way.' He gave the Lysander a final push. 'Anyway, sorry about the gas mask, and all that. I'll sort some comics out for you, shall I?'

Colin listened to his footsteps going downstairs. Seven years he'd known Adrian. He could remember the first time they'd met. Orange-boxes in the living room, Viv irritable, wanting him out of the way. Nobody in the street to play with. Then Adrian came home, and they'd played snakes and ladders on the table in the kitchen, and for the first time in Colin's life, he'd wanted somebody else to win.

What he didn't remember was when he'd first realized that Adrian's father was dead. Because that was the real bond, for him certainly, and he thought for Adrian too, though it was difficult to be sure what Adrian felt about anything. He'd never talked about his father. Never once, in all those years.

Colin lay and watched the Lysander turn slowly on the end of its string. On the wall behind it, the sunlight had cast a pale shadow that swayed as the plane swayed.

Sometimes the shadow vanished altogether, as the room chilled, but always the silver-grey outline reappeared, darkening to charcoal, and finally to black, as the sun struggled clear. And whenever this happened, the shadow seemed more solid than the plane.

Pierre, Maurice and Bernard are sitting at the table, drinking wine. Bernard is dressed as a man, and seems different, older. Paulette comes in, carrying a tray.

PAULETTE

Says he's too ill to get up.

BERNARD

How convenient for him.

PIERRE

Not just for him. Close the door, Paulette.

She closes the door, and comes to sit at the table. The four heads bend in close, and they speak in whispers . . .

BERNARD

What do you intend to do?

PIERRE

You're in charge, Bernard.

BERNARD

I'm blown, useless. You know I am.

PAULETTE

We all are. Thanks to him.

Are we? Correct me if I'm wrong, Maurice, but Gaston has never actually met you?

MAURICE

No, he hasn't.

BERNARD

He knows the codename, but nothing more.

MAURICE

So?

PIERRE

So you're the one who's going to spill the beans to the Gestapo.

They all stare at him.

You're going to denounce Gaston.

MAURICE

What good will that do? Do you think they don't know their own agents?

PIERRE

They know him in this area, yes, but not in yours. And they're not going to waste time checking. They'll act on the information you give them as soon as they get it.

MAURICE

And how do we persuade Gaston to come into my area?

PIERRE

That won't be difficult. As soon as he's stopped faking this illness.

He glances contemptuously at the ceiling.

I'll tell him there are some secret documents to be collected. He won't be able to resist that. In fact I'm so certain of him, I've got his identity papers ready.

He pulls an identity card out of his pocket and hands it round. Paulette frowns as she examines it.

PAULETTE

But this is useless. He'd never get past a checkpoint with this.

PIERRE

I know.

He smiles.

You see, my dear, *we*'re not going to kill Gaston. *They* are.

The wind had dropped. The Lysander hung motionless from the end of its string. Colin felt the house draw in on itself, cradle itself, as people do when they've been terribly injured.

He got out of bed and went on to the landing, hanging over the banisters to listen. No sound from the kitchen. No sound from the Hennigans' flat either, though on Adrian's days off, that was usually noisy.

He tiptoed downstairs, and opened the kitchen door.

Pierre, Bernard and Paulette look up as Gaston comes in. From the sudden silence, it's clear they've been talking about him.

The fourth chair is now occupied, not by Maurice, but by Vivienne, who is dramatically and unmistakably dead. Nobody pays the slightest attention to her, except Gaston, whose eyes are continually pulled in that direction, though he tries to behave as if nothing is wrong.

PIERRE

Ah, Gaston, you're looking a lot better. Isn't he, Bernard?

BERNARD

Back to normal, I'd say.

PAULETTE

He doesn't look normal to me.

In fact, Gaston has the shifty-eyed look of somebody on the edge of hallucination.

GASTON

I'm all right.

BERNARD

Of course you are. You can't wait to get your hands on those documents, can you? Such dedication to the cause.

PIERRE
(*holding out an envelope*)

Here's your identity card, Gaston.

GASTON

Well, actually, I've been thinking about that. Oh, don't get me wrong, I want to go . . . But I was just wondering if it has to be *today*. I thought I might go out, get a breath of fresh air. I've been cooped up in that room for days . . .

His voice edges up into hysteria. He keeps glancing at the chair where Vivienne sits.

PIERRE
(*smoothly*)

No, I'm afraid it has to be today. We need the documents urgently.

PAULETTE

If you're not well enough, I'll go.

BERNARD

You can't let a *girl* do it.

All right! I'll go.

He begins to walk across to the table, to collect his identity card, but the table seems a long way away. Pierre is telling Gaston where to go to find the documents, but his voice booms and diminishes like a train entering and leaving a tunnel, and his face is elongated, the forehead unnaturally domed.

I can't . . .

He stumbles against the side of the table.

'Well, if you can't, don't. You're supposed to be in bed anyway.'

Viv shoved him into one of the chairs around the table, and sat down herself, in the chair occupied a few seconds earlier by the dead Vivienne.

'Have I got a smut on me nose, or something? Colin, what's wrong?'

He tried to pull himself together. 'Nothing.'

'Here, have a cup of tea.'

He knew the tea was a mistake, as soon as he started to drink, but he forced himself to go on, because Viv had made it and he owed her that at least.

'You *are* going to work, aren't you?' he asked.

'Depends. I was gunna go downstairs and ask Mrs Hennigan if she'd sit with you, but then I thought I'd wait for Pauline. It's Pauline's night off, you see. Only I don't know whether she's got anything planned.'

'I'll be all right on me own. I'm not helpless, you know.'

'No, I know you're not. You've not been brought up to be helpless, have you, son?'

She smiled at him, a little wryly perhaps, and he smiled back.

'Come on now, up to bed.'

They'd reached the landing before he vomited. Bile scalding the inside of his nose, he said, 'I'm sorry, Mam.'

'I've cleaned up worse. Go on, get into bed.'

He started to shiver as soon as his skin touched the sheets. Viv came in with clean pyjamas, and a hot-water bottle wrapped in a towel. She helped him change, then slid the hot-water bottle under his knees. 'There,' she said. 'You'll soon warm up. If I was you, I'd try and have a little sleep.'

But he couldn't sleep. For a while, he tried to look at the picures in his film annuals, but all the films were jumbled together in his head. He was tired of them anyway: the clipped, courageous voices, the thoroughly decent chaps, the British bombs that always landed on target, the British bomb-ers that always managed to limp home. They told lies, he thought. They said it was easy to be brave.

He needed a pee, and he wasn't going to ask Viv for help. In a series of little rushes, from one piece of furniture to the next, he struggled from the bedroom to the bathroom.

His urine was thick, orange-coloured. The smell made him feel sick. He sat on the edge of the bath, when he'd finished, the rim a cold bar across his hot thighs, and braced himself for the long journey back to bed.

He got as far as the landing, then stopped and looked over the banister. The silence was back. Only now it wasn't just downstairs: the bedrooms behind him felt hollow.

He opened Viv's door.

The room was empty, not just of people, but of things as well. Even the curtains were gone. Only a square of lace, stiff with dirt, shielded the room from the sky.

He went in, his footsteps sounding on the bare boards, and looked around. Lighter patches of wallpaper showed where the wardrobe and bed had been. He crossed to the window. Grass grew on the bare patch where Adrian's bike had stood. The shed had a hole in the roof.

He wasn't afraid, though he knew he ought to be. He listened. No sound came from the street. No sound from inside the house either, except this endless, singing, audible silence. And then — footsteps. The creak of a floorboard. Somebody was climbing the stairs.

Colin turned to face the door. The footsteps crossed the landing, slowly, but not hesitantly. He knew the way.

His shadow darkened the doorway. And then he was in the room, staring, as Colin had stared, at the lighter patches on the wallpaper. He turned towards the window, and Colin opened his mouth to speak, but the eyes passed over him, unseeing.

He was wearing a black suit, and a black tie. He looked out of place in the dingy room, and not merely because it was empty. He could surely never have belonged here. And yet he looked as if he knew it.

He went across to the place where the bed had been, and stood looking down. He said, in a self-conscious, almost experimental tone, '*Mam*?'

Colin backed away. He told himself this was a dream, and soon he would wake up, and all the while he knew he wasn't dreaming. This was more terrifying than any nightmare could have been. He was seeing his own ghost.

He moved, and the man glanced in his direction, as if for a moment he thought he'd seen a shadow flit between him and the light. Then he smiled, and said: ' "... *it is but a child of air that lingers in the garden there* ..." '

Child of air — *ballocks*, Colin thought. He didn't like this man. He didn't like his eyes. He didn't like the thin, over-sensitive mouth. Above all, he didn't like the way he'd said 'Mam' as if it was a word in a foreign language.

'You are not me,' Colin said.

A flicker of fear, but it faded. The man looked round the room again, as if searching for something, but for something inside himself, Colin thought. For something he ought to feel, and couldn't.

Colin started to walk towards him. The man couldn't see, he couldn't hear, there was no way of challenging him, that Colin could think of, except to stand where he stood, to occupy the space he claimed as his. It would be all right, Colin thought, as long as his nerve didn't break, as long as he didn't let the horror of looking into his own face overpower him. A few inches away, he stopped.

Only one of them would walk away, and Colin realized, at the last moment, that he didn't know which. He stepped forward. He didn't know what he'd expected, perhaps a slight chill, a jolt, a shock even, but he felt none of these things. Just the faint brush of air against his skin, and then he was alone, in the blanched silence of his mother's room, with all the furniture back.

18

'Mam?'

'Yeh?'

'Have you ever thought every year we live through the day of our own deaths?'

Viv lowered her cup. 'No, I haven't. Aw, Colin, what a morbid thought. Look, you've given me the shivers.' She rubbed her bare arm, fiercely. 'Anyway, I hope you don't think *you*'re dying, 'cause you're not.'

'No, I know I'm not. Didn't mean that.'

He'd meant *her* death, of course. He was still trying to come up with an explanation, not for his seeing the man, because he knew that couldn't be explained, but for the black suit and tie. Though if he didn't accept the man was him, Viv's death could have nothing to do with it.

'I wish you'd stop staring at me, Colin. I'm beginning to think I must have two heads.'

'No,' he said. 'I'm just glad you're here.'

She reared away. 'Yeh, I am here, and I shouldn't be, look at the time. Pauline said she'd be here by now.'

The doorbell rang.

'That'll be her now,' he said.

'Right, I'm off.' She bent to kiss him, an almost unheard of event. 'Now don't you have her running up and down stairs all night. Remember it's supposed to be her night off.'

He listened to the tap of her heels on the stairs, and then to their voices talking together. After a while he turned over on to his side, and faced the window.

—*I hope you don't think you're dying. I hope you don't think you're dying. I hope you don't . . .*

The steam from a departing train clears to reveal German guards waiting at the barrier. French civilians, among them Gaston, queue to present their identity cards.

Gaston keeps fingering a bundle of papers in the inside pocket of his jacket. Obviously, he wasn't expecting this check. The guard takes his time, looking from each card to the person offering it, and back again. Gaston examines his own identity card, and frowns, as he picks out the flaws.

Gaston looks round for a way of escape. On the opposite platform, a man lowers his newspaper. Pierre. Gaston looks past the barrier, and the man queuing for a ticket turns round. Bernard. Neither Pierre nor Bernard shows any sign of recognition.

Gaston's eyes focus on the guard's hand, as it reaches out to take the identity card of the woman in front. Fear begins to break up the smooth planes of his face. He turns and runs.

Achtung! Achtung!

But Gaston is beyond hearing. Rifle-fire cracks out, civilians scatter, and Gaston throws up his arms, caught like a runner breasting the tape, and held there for a moment before he slowly falls.

Pigeons, startled by the shots, batter their wings against the glass roof of the station, until at last, finding a way out, they stream into the upper air.

Pauline took the thermometer out of his mouth.

'Down,' she said. 'And I don't think that arm looks as bad either. How does it feel?'

Colin flexed his shoulder. 'All right.'

Pauline leant across the bed. Colin realized, in a rush of blood and shyness, that she was pretty, very pretty, even if she was old enough to be his mother's friend.

She touched his neck. 'I can't feel any swelling.'

She would if she leant any further over.

'Back to school on Monday.'

'*No.*'

She laughed. 'I thought that'd make you sit up.'

Colin hesitated. 'Pauline . . .'

'Hm?'

'You know I was asking you what you did in the war? Well, there was a reason.'

'Was there?'

He saw her lips twitch.

'Oh, I see,' he said. 'Transparent?'

'No-o, not *transparent*. It did cross me mind it might have something to do with your father.'

'I just thought you might know.'

'I'm sorry, Colin, I don't.'

'She didn't tell you?'

'No.'

He kept his voice casual. 'Oh, well, that's that, then.'

'You'll just have to keep on asking, Colin.'

'She doesn't bloody well *know*!'

A pause.

'That's a hard thing to say, Colin.'

'What else am I supposed to think?'

A pause.

'Well, love, all I can say is, There was a war on. People grabbed what they could. I know I did.' She put her hands on her knees and stood up. 'Look, I'm going to make a cup of tea. Do you want me to bring you one up?'

'Yes, please.'

So the blank space would remain blank, he thought. Well, he could live with that. People had survived far worse.

He looked at the Lysander, as it swayed gently on the end of its string. Suddenly, his eyes gleamed. He began making aeroplane noises, softly at first, then louder . . .

Night. An improvised landing strip. Bernard, Pierre and Paulette are crouching in the shadow of some bushes, listening to the drone of an aeroplane, coming closer.

PAULETTE

Listen, that's it, now. Thank God.

PIERRE

Thank Him when we're on the other side of the Channel. I wish you'd change your mind and come with us, Bernard.

BERNARD

No, I've made up my mind. Don't worry, I'll be all right. I've survived worse than this.

Pierre glances at Paulette, then draws Bernard a little to one side.

Bernard . . . There's something that's always . . . worried me. All this dressing as a woman – you do do it just for France?

Bernard smiles.

Suddenly, all three are forced to clutch their heads and bend away from the roar. The bushes whiten as the blast from the plane tosses their branches about, and reveals the underside of their leaves. Out of the night sky, the Lysander swoops down to meet its shadow.

No time for goodbyes. Two figures detach themselves from the bushes and run towards the plane.

Inside the cockpit, the pilot mimes a welcome, but Paulette and Pierre go at once to the window, and look down.

Alone in the windswept clearing, Bernard looks up and waves. He watches as the Lysander banks steeply, and heads towards the Channel, dwindling, in a matter of seconds, to the size of a toy plane.

Then he turns up the collar of his coat and slips away into the darkness.

Colin, staring straight ahead, waited for the drone of the Lysander to fade. Then he gave a sharp, decisive little nod, and said, 'The End'.